"So can we stay the week?"

The sun glinted on Summer's hair. For the first time since losing his wife, Jake felt the pull of attraction.

He stifled it immediately. He'd made a firm decision to stay away from women after what he'd done. This was the first time he'd felt any inkling of wanting to break that vow.

But he guessed he could handle Summer and her kids' presence for a week.

"You can stay," he said, "if your references check out."

"Thank you!" For a minute, he thought she was going to hug him, but she just smiled broadly and started looking around the kitchen. "I really appreciate it, and I promise you, we'll leave things better than they were. Hopefully including your dad. If it's okay with you, I'll start with tidying up and cleaning in here."

He felt good that he'd put the happiness back into her face.

He just needed to make sure he didn't get too carried away with enjoying making her happy. That was something he was determined to resist.

Lee Tobin McClain is the *New York Times* bestselling author of emotional small-town romances featuring flawed characters who find healing through friendship, faith and family. Lee grew up in Ohio and now lives in Western Pennsylvania, where she enjoys hiking with her goofy goldendoodle, visiting writer friends and admiring her daughter's mastery of the latest TikTok dances. Learn more about her books at leetobinmcclain.com.

Books by Lee Tobin McClain

Love Inspired

Holiday Haven

A Home for Mother's Day

Tumbleweed, Texas

The Coach's Secret Child

K-9 Companions

Her Easter Prayer
The Veteran's Holiday Home
A Friend to Trust
A Companion for Christmas
A Companion for His Son
His Christmas Salvation
The Veteran's Valentine Helper
Holding Onto Secrets
Her Surprise Neighbor
An Unexpected Christmas Helper

Rescue Haven

The Secret Christmas Child
Child on His Doorstep
Finding a Christmas Home

Visit the Author Profile page at LoveInspired.com for more titles.

A HOME FOR MOTHER'S DAY

LEE TOBIN McCLAIN

LOVE INSPIRED
INSPIRATIONAL ROMANCE

FSC www.fsc.org
MIX
Paper | Supporting responsible forestry
FSC® C021394

LOVE INSPIRED®
INSPIRATIONAL ROMANCE

Please recycle
This product is recyclable
Recycling programs for this product may not exist in your area.

ISBN-13: 978-1-335-62153-5

A Home for Mother's Day

For questions and comments about the quality of this book, please contact us at CustomerService@Harlequin.com.

® is a trademark of Harlequin Enterprises ULC.

Love Inspired
22 Adelaide St. West, 41st Floor
Toronto, Ontario M5H 4E3, Canada
www.LoveInspired.com

HarperCollins Publishers
Macken House, 39/40 Mayor Street Upper,
Dublin 1, D01 C9W8, Ireland
www.HarperCollins.com

Printed in Lithuania

Two are better than one; because they have a good reward for their labour. For if they fall, the one will lift up his fellow: but woe to him that is alone when he falleth; for he hath not another to help him up.

—*Ecclesiastes* 4:9–10

To Bill, whose enthusiasm for
fishing and the Yough River inspired this book.

Chapter One

Summer Jones parked her ancient Volkswagen van in front of the Holiday Haven Guesthouse. Her shoulders sagged with relief. They'd made it.

"We're staying *here* for vacation?" Beside her, ten-year-old Wyatt crossed his arms and glared.

"Yes, and it's going to be great!" Summer didn't have to dig too deep to find a smile. She'd had such fun times at the Holiday Haven Guesthouse as a kid. She hoped a vacation here would help her own kids get past the last six miserable months and enjoy a happy, healthy spring break.

Rylee, her four-year-old, stirred in the back seat. She'd been asleep most of the two-hour drive from their Pittsburgh home.

Former home, Summer reminded herself.

"Are we there?" Rylee asked. "Mommy? Are we there?"

"Yes, we're here!" Summer reached back and patted her daughter's leg.

"And it's a dump," Wyatt grouched.

As Summer watched the last sliver of sun disappear behind the guesthouse, worry pushed its way past her determined cheerfulness. The Holiday Haven sign was faded, and random weeds sprouted in what had used to be pretty flower gardens.

But the structure was the same as she remembered: a sprawling building with several additions complete with their own front porches. Through an open walkway that connected two halves of the building, she could see the large deck and beyond that, the river.

"Look, the river runs right past the backyard," she said to Wyatt. "You can fish there!"

Wyatt brightened, and then his face fell. "Aw, I don't have any bait. And I didn't bring my rod."

"The guesthouse might have one you can borrow," Summer told him. "And there's a little grocery just down the road. I'm sure they carry bait. If they're closed, you can try digging for worms." She wasn't sure how late a small-town grocery store would be open.

"Okay." Wyatt opened his car door.

Summer climbed out and opened the van's back door for Rylee. Despite the cheerfulness she'd displayed to the kids, her stomach was starting to hurt. The guesthouse's website had been antiquated. Had she ever gotten an email confirmation? Things had been so hectic, she couldn't remember for sure. All she knew was that the price had been amazingly low. A blast from the past.

This had to work. If not, they'd spend the week camping in the van. That was Plan B, but with two young city kids, the Holiday Haven Guesthouse would definitely be better.

Wyatt started to pull his suitcase from the back of the van, but she stopped him. "Let's check it out first, before we bring our bags." She led him and Rylee toward the guesthouse and knocked at the door marked Office.

There was no response.

She knocked again, harder, causing chips of paint to fall to the ground. When no one came, she tried ringing the doorbell, her heart sinking.

"What if nobody's home?" Rylee tightened her grip on Summer's hand.

Suddenly the door opened.

Summer blinked at the stooped, gray-haired man who stood in front of her. It took a minute to realize that this was the same man who'd run the place when she'd come here as a kid. He was dressed neatly in jeans and a chambray shirt, but his expression wasn't that of a host expecting a guest.

"Hi, Mr. Wright," she said through the screen. "I stayed here a long time ago, several times, and wanted to bring my kids to have a vacation here like I did. We have a reservation."

"Well, I don't think you do," he said. He didn't look unfriendly, just kind of puzzled.

"I made it online a couple of days ago."

He opened the door and stepped outside. "I don't do online."

Summer kept smiling with an effort, knowing her kids were looking to her for guidance. Night would fall soon. Finding a place to camp would be a challenge, here in the hills of Southwestern Pennsylvania.

"Aw, man." Wyatt's shoulders hunched.

"Can't we *please* stay here?" Rylee looked up at the man with the same winning smile she used to try to wheedle treats out of their elderly neighbor back home.

Mr. Wright squinted at Wyatt and Rylee. "You can stay, I guess. Come on around. Which suite did you want?"

This seemed unorthodox, but given her options, she decided to at least check out the place. "We reserved the second-floor one with two bedrooms and a river view," she said.

"That's fine, then. My son lives in the front suite, and I'm behind the office. All the other rooms are empty."

Summer's heart sank. "Are you even open?" she asked,

but Mr. Wright was climbing the outdoor stairs and didn't seem to hear her. He produced a key from the ledge above the transom and let them in.

They walked into the suite's front room. The furniture was covered with sheets and the curtains were closed. Dust coated every surface, and the place smelled musty. "We need to find you some sheets and towels," the old man said. "Mama wouldn't like how dirty it is. People won't pay for dirt, she always said."

Rylee leaned against Summer's side. Wyatt crossed his arms and frowned.

Summer's mind raced through alternatives, something she'd gotten accustomed to doing ever since her so-called husband had dropped his bombshell. "I can clean it for you," she said, "if we can stay for a reduced price. And borrow a fishing rod."

Mr. Wright looked around the room, his mouth twisting to one side. "You can stay for free, if you really want to. Too much of a mess to charge you. Fishing rods are in the shed out back."

"Can he dig for worms?" Summer bargained, nodding at Wyatt.

"Sure can. We've had a lot of rain." He half smiled at Wyatt. "I'll show you where to dig."

"Terrific! Kids, let's bring in our bags." At least this was better than sleeping in the van. She had to get used to improvising. So did her kids. "This is going to be fun!"

They fetched their bags and brought them upstairs, Mr. Wright helping them. He pointed out a closet where linens and cleaning supplies could be found and then disappeared with Wyatt, who was chattering about the fishing he'd done in Pittsburgh's Highland Park.

"Let's set up the girls' room first, for you and me," she said to Rylee. "You can help clean."

They opened windows to air out the place and spread sheets on the twin beds. Rylee imitated Summer, patting at the sheets. Then, she accidentally tugged them off-center. She was basically undoing Summer's work, but that was a four-year-old. Summer didn't mind. Whatever made her anxious daughter happy.

Summer was just starting to sweep the floor, with Rylee holding the dustpan, when the suite door opened. "What's going on in here?" a stern male voice asked.

Rylee rushed to Summer and lifted her hands to be picked up, as if she were still a toddler.

Summer turned to look at the man who'd invaded their space. Tall and broad-shouldered, he wore jeans, a flannel shirt and a very grumpy expression.

She should have known this had been too easy.

Jake Wright waited for the intruder to answer his question. When she didn't, instead stroking her daughter's hair back and murmuring soothing nothings, he repeated it. "What's going on?"

He'd gotten an uneasy feeling when he'd seen that van parked in front of the place, full of suitcases and sleeping bags and boxes of food. He'd figured it belonged to a squatter; he just hadn't expected the squatter to be so pretty.

"We're staying here," she said, lifting her chin.

"No, you're not. Where's my father?" His dad was the priority. He needed to make sure Dad was safe and get rid of this threat, ASAP.

The little girl buried her face in her mother's shoulder and started to cry.

Jake restrained an eye roll just in case the little girl was truly upset. More likely, the woman had pinched her to make her cry and play on his sympathy. "Clear out," he said.

The little girl cried harder.

"Your dad's outside with my son." She shifted the little girl to her other hip. "He said we could stay. You can ask him."

"Fine, but you're coming with me," he said. No way was he leaving them alone in the guesthouse. "This way." He ushered them out of the suite and then led the way past the other, empty rooms and suites, and then down the stairs. They walked through the common living room, past the kitchen, and out to the big back deck.

The sun was an orange ball in the sky, half-hidden behind the trees that were just starting to leaf up. There, at the edge of the river, he saw his father and a young boy, fishing.

It reminded him of when he and Dad had fished together, back in happier days. He pushed away the memory because it hurt his heart. He was supposed to take care of his father, protect him. If these interlopers had gotten to Dad so easily, then he wasn't doing a very good job.

"I'm Summer Jones, and this is my daughter, Rylee. That's Wyatt, down there with your dad." She looked at him expectantly.

"Jake Wright." He didn't say he was pleased to meet her, because he wasn't.

The woman tried to put down the little girl, but she clung on. "Do we hafta leave?" she asked in a shaky voice.

"Don't you worry about that," Summer said in a warm voice, and then gave the girl a loud, smacking kiss on the cheek. "It's a grown-up problem, and grown-ups will fix it. Why don't you run down and see if Wyatt's caught anything?"

Just then, the boy's rod bent, and he whooped. The little

girl, Rylee, ran toward the river. She squatted down on the dock beside the area where they'd been fishing. Jake craned his neck to make sure the rowboat was securely tied. It was.

"River's shallow right at the banks, but it gets deep fast," Jake said to the mom. Summer, she'd said her name was. "Make sure she doesn't go to the end of the dock."

"Stay there, Rylee," Summer called. "No further."

The little girl nodded without taking her eyes off her brother.

"Reel him in." Dad set down his own rod. A fish jumped at the end of the boy's line, and Dad grabbed a net and walked over. The little girl started jumping up and down.

Jake walked closer, the woman beside him. He'd have expected her to make a lot of noise—women tended to do that—but she kept quiet and watched, a little smile on her face.

The boy reeled in the fish, and Dad reached out and netted it. Jake caught himself rooting for the kid, hoping the fish—looked like a trout, a big one—wouldn't escape and wiggle back into the water.

The little girl ran off the dock and hid behind her brother, squealing a little, as Dad set the thrashing creature on the grassy shoreline. He knelt down and talked to both kids.

When was the last time Dad had talked to a stranger? It had to have been weeks ago.

"It's catch and release for trout at this time of year," Jake said, watching the fish flop on the grass.

"You'll have to let it go, Wyatt," the woman called, and the boy looked back and nodded.

Dad started taking the hook out as both kids watched.

Jake turned to the woman. Sure, she had cute kids, and his dad seemed to be enjoying himself, which didn't happen often these days. Still, Jake wasn't going to be taken in. "Like I said inside, you'll have to leave."

"Nope." She crossed her arms. "Your dad said we could stay for free if we'd clean the suite. Which is a bargain for him, if you ask me."

Jake frowned. He knew all the rooms were dirty. No one had aired them out or cleaned them since Mom had gotten sick. He should have done it, but he hadn't had the bandwidth, what with keeping the auto shop going.

"Just how did you find us?" he asked, watching as his father gestured toward the water. The boy picked the fish up, gingerly, and placed it carefully in the water just as Dad had taught Jake to do, many years ago. Then the boy pulled his hands back, and both kids stared into the water, obviously fascinated to watch the fish swim away.

"I used to stay here," she said, glancing back at the guesthouse, a smile on her face. "When I was a kid. So we made a reservation online, and here we are."

Jake puffed out a disgusted breath. "That site hasn't been updated in years," he said.

"Then it should be taken down. We have a right to stay." She looked at him with a stubborn expression. Then she glanced down toward the river and bit her lip. "Plus, we have nowhere else to go tonight."

"Not my problem." Jake tried not to look at the kids. Tried not to look at her worried face.

She didn't say anything.

He gazed out to the river, to the trees on the other side. A shore bird swooped over the water, looking for dinner. The night breeze was cool. A train chugged by behind them, on the tracks across the road from the guesthouse, blowing its whistle.

He watched his dad, who'd knelt beside the little girl,

pointing out at the river. Dad had no problem being kind to these children. Why was Jake so reluctant?

But he knew why. He hadn't let himself get close to a pretty woman, let alone one with cute kids, since his pregnant wife had driven her car into a tree eight years ago.

"Look, Mister," the woman said quietly. "My son is happy for the first time in weeks. I would really, really appreciate if you'd let us stay, at least for tonight."

Jake glanced down at the boy, who was picking up his sister. Dad gathered up the rods, the net and his tackle box and headed for the shed.

The boy carried his sister over, staggering a little, and put her down beside her mother. "Did you see the fish I caught?"

"I did!" She gave him a quick hug. "That was amazing!"

She listened to her son describe in detail how he'd reeled in the fish. She'd just seen it happen, as Jake had, but she encouraged the boy with questions. The little girl, Rylee, chimed in with admiration of the giant fish her brother had caught.

Maybe Summer was just ditzy and goofy, not conniving. And the kids seemed not only cute, but sweet, supportive of each other even at their young ages. It reminded Jake of his connection with his own younger sister, right next door.

When the boy finished his story, the little girl spoke up, pointing at Jake. "That man says we can't stay here."

The little boy's face fell. The woman pressed her lips together.

Was he really going to be that much of a jerk? To hear his late wife, probably so. He'd been a terrible partner, a terrible person.

But Jake was trying to be better. At least a little more kind and caring.

At the same time, he was committed to protecting his father and sister in a way he hadn't protected his wife and unborn child. That was what he lived for, these days.

He looked again into the kids' faces. "I guess you can stay the night." And he would keep an eye on them, especially the pretty mom.

If she did anything that could hurt his dad or his sister, she and her kids would be out of here as fast as Jake could push them.

•

The next morning Summer was downstairs by 6:00 a.m., a broom, mop and bucket in hand.

Last night, she'd stayed up late cleaning the suite where they'd stayed. After five hours of tossing and turning, she'd jumped up and hurried downstairs, leaving both kids sound asleep.

This was her chance to make herself so useful to Mr. Wright and his scowling son that they'd agree she and the kids could stay for the week. They needed it, especially Wyatt. She wanted desperately to keep that happy expression she'd seen last night on his face.

The glass-fronted kitchen cupboards held pasta and cans of soup, and there were milk, eggs and a bag of apples in the refrigerator, along with a couple of take-out containers. So this must still be the main kitchen, the one Mr. Wright and his son used.

When she'd stayed here with her parents long ago, they'd occasionally eaten out at restaurants or grilled dinner outside. But they, along with all the other guests, had been welcome to share Mr. and Mrs. Wright's big kitchen whenever they'd wanted to. She still remembered the fancy homemade cookies that pretty, long-haired, barefooted Mrs. Wright had set out in a canister labeled Help Yourself.

The Wrights had treated their guests like family. That was

why people had flocked here for holidays, especially smaller families like her own, or single people, or elderly couples. Christmas dinners and Fourth of July barbeques had been part of the appeal. The Wrights had seemed to love sharing their home with strangers.

Apparently, their son hadn't inherited the hospitality gene. Come to think of it, she remembered there had been a cute teenage son in the family, although he'd been enough older that they hadn't had more than a few passing interactions.

She inspected the kitchen, considering where to start.

The big table in the center of the room was dusty except for one end, where plastic place mats and two high-backed wooden chairs suggested recent use. She wiped down the table, swept the floor and then filled the bucket at the big kitchen sink and squirted in some pine-scented cleanser. The linoleum's built-in grime might take some elbow grease to remove, but it was cheerful, honest work.

She emptied the dustpan into the big trash bin, noticed it didn't smell great, and added that to her mental list. There was more than a week's worth of cleaning to do right here in this kitchen, she suspected.

Her phone buzzed and she grabbed it. When she saw "Chuck" on the lock screen, she froze.

Should she take it? She hadn't spoken to her ex in weeks, didn't want to hear his voice. But she suspected she knew what this call was about. Best to get it over with.

As soon as she answered, he started talking rapidly in a low voice. "You turned the keys for the house over to the bank. What on earth were you thinking, Summer?"

The sound of Chuck's voice made her heart skip a little, but his words took away any remnant of warmth inside her. No *hello*, no *how are you*, no *how are the kids*. Just business. "I couldn't pay the mortgage," she said. "It was that or foreclosure, which would have killed both our credit scores."

"You should have contacted me."

"I tried. You must have been too busy with your *other* family."

He ignored her snarky tone. "Where are you staying now? Where are the kids?"

"None of your business." She swirled a hand in the bucket to mix in the cleaning liquid, making cloudy bubbles.

"You need to keep me informed," he said.

"Actually, I have no legal obligation to you whatsoever." She lifted the bucket out of the sink and onto the floor, then dipped in the sponge mop. She set down the phone and put it on speaker, then started mopping. The floor was actually bright white underneath the grime. Satisfying.

"Hold on a minute," he said.

She ought to hang up on him, but there was some sense of responsibility lingering. She'd once loved this man, and he was the father of her children. She mopped vigorously, dipping the mop every few strokes. Soon the water was gray, so she dumped it and refilled the bucket.

"Are you there?" came Chuck's voice from the phone. "What are you doing? I hear water running. Where are you living now?"

She didn't want him to know where they were. "I'm mopping the floor. Trying to ingratiate myself to our hosts so we can stay here, since I'm totally broke."

Silence from the phone. She started scrubbing a new section of the floor, hard.

"Tell the kids I love them," he said.

That tugged at her heart, because she knew it was true. They loved him, too.

"Dad!" came a teen's voice from the phone. A younger child chimed in. "Daddy, we need you."

Her heart went stone cold. She leaned against the counter, her heart pounding so hard she thought it might burst. "Go see to your kids," she choked out, and ended the call. She grabbed a rag and started scrubbing the floor on her hands and knees, hard.

She'd known he had another family. He'd left her and the kids to be with them. But to have it rubbed in her face like that, to hear his other kids calling him Dad…yeah. That was why she wanted to limit Wyatt and Rylee's exposure to him. They'd be devastated if they heard what she'd just heard.

The squeak of the kitchen door was her only warning, and then a pair of legs approached her. She looked up to see Jake, arms crossed, mouth twisted to one side. "I overheard part of your phone call. You may be able to ingratiate yourself with my father, but it won't work with me."

Chapter Two

After he'd told off Summer, Jake retreated to his suite to get ready for church.

He didn't feel satisfied like he'd expected. He'd awakened this morning intending to boot her out today. Why had he even let her stay? Yeah, her kids were cute, and yeah, they'd cheered Dad up, but that was no reason to reopen the guesthouse. It was too much for Dad to run alone, and so they'd let the business die when Mom had gotten sick. Jake himself had had his hands full keeping up the family's auto repair shop right next door. And Kitty, his sister, was a single mom and taught school full time. No way could she take on running the guesthouse.

So he'd let Summer know she needed to be out by the end of the day. Her eyes had welled up with tears, but she hadn't denied what he'd overheard her say on the phone: she openly admitted she *was* trying to ingratiate herself with him and his dad so they'd let her little family stay the week.

She'd insisted on finishing the kitchen floor. He had to admit, it hadn't looked this clean since Mom had been healthy.

As he buttoned his dress shirt, Jake heard a shout from Summer's suite.

"I'm not going to church!"

He stopped, tilted his head. He heard her low, husky response, but he couldn't detect what she was saying.

"We're on vacation!" her son yelled.

There were more calm words, then a higher voice from the little girl. He didn't even remember their names. Didn't intend to learn them, either. The family was leaving today.

He combed his hair and went down the hall to his father's suite. He tapped the door. "Dad?"

"Just a minute," his father grumbled.

While he waited, Jake looked around the musty, dusty hallway and thought what the place must look like to an outsider. It was actually pretty surprising she'd been willing to stay here with her kids. She must be desperate.

The door opened, and Jake's heart sank when he saw his father's droopy eyes, beard stubble and old flannel shirt. "I'm not going," Dad rasped out.

Jake thought of Summer, her low, calm voice. "It would be good for you to get out to church," he said.

"No. You go ahead." Dad closed the door, gently but firmly.

Jake sighed and headed out. His father was an adult and got to make his own choices, but Jake couldn't help but worry. In the six months since Mom had died, Dad rarely went anywhere, not even to check on the auto business he'd founded. If something didn't improve, Jake would have to see about getting Dad some counseling. Which he dreaded—they really didn't *do* counseling in his family—but he knew that depression like Dad's could be dangerous.

A sudden rain shower drummed against the porch roof. Jake had intended to walk—their church, situated in the middle of town, wasn't half a mile away—but due to the weather, he sprinted to his truck. As soon as he was inside and had it started up, he saw Summer and her kids climbing into the VW van. So she'd won the battle with her son about church. Good.

He was heading out when he heard a grinding sound as the van started. Then it died. Sounded like an issue with the engine, which wouldn't be surprising given the age of the vehicle.

Not my problem, he told himself. But he pulled over to the side of the road and watched in his rearview mirror.

Summer got out in her cute dress and tall boots, a wide-brimmed hat her only protection from the rain. She opened the rear hatch. That in itself was surprising, but if you drove a vintage vehicle, you had to learn to at least diagnose problems.

Jake couldn't see what she was doing to the engine, but he saw her walk around to the side doors of the van and pull out an oil can.

The boy got out and said something, looking triumphant.

She spoke with him, her shoulders slumping a little, and walked toward the back of the camper van.

He wanted to drive on, but his conscience wouldn't let him. He backed up and stopped beside the van. "Need a ride to church?"

Her eyes widened and her face broke into a wide, dimpled smile. Maybe the prettiest smile he'd ever seen. "That would be great. Come on, kids."

Jake got out and moved a few things off the truck's back seat. The kids climbed in, the boy pouting, the girl endearing in her bright pink skirt and sweater. So they'd brought church clothes.

As he held the door for Summer, he glanced back toward her van. It was packed to the gills, as if they were moving, not just taking a vacation. That seemed like a red flag. He'd take them to church, but afterward, they were out of here.

* * *

Two hours later, they were back at the guesthouse. The sun was shining now—typical Western Pennsylvania springtime—and the temperature had to be in the high sixties.

He could hear his sister inside the guesthouse, singing along to the radio. That was good. Dad had some company, and the tantalizing fragrance of Kitty's fried chicken wafted toward him. The kids whooped as they got out of the truck, something about ducks, and ran down toward the river.

"Wait—" Summer started, then shrugged. "Oh, well, shoes can be cleaned. I'll let them run."

"They were well behaved in church." Jake had sat with them, because it would have seemed unfriendly not to, even though it would no doubt cause some gossip. Even the four-year-old had been quiet, if a little wiggly. They'd been no hindrance to Jake listening to the message.

Summer, sitting there rapt, her makeup-free face shining, had been more of a distraction than the kids.

That, he could do without. But attending services had made him feel bad about his lack of charity. Summer was clearly trying. It wasn't her fault that the guesthouse wasn't set up for visitors.

It *was* her fault that they'd come here. She should have checked into things more carefully before dragging her kids to a defunct place. But it was his fault, too. He should have made sure the old website was taken down.

"Thanks so much for the ride," Summer said now. She started toward her kids.

"Just a minute." Jake's sister, Kitty, came out in jeans and an apron. She was spotty about going to church, but she did come over to the guesthouse most Sundays. Brought her son, usually, but from the silence, he suspected Mason was with his dad's parents for a visit.

Kitty stepped in front of Summer. "Dad said you talked him into letting you stay here." She shot a glare at Jake. The message was clear: he should have stopped it from happening.

"That's on me," Jake said quickly. "I let Summer and her kids stay the night, since they got here late, but they'll be heading out today."

Summer twisted a piece of hair. "I should have checked into things before I got here," she said to Kitty. "I just, I had great memories of staying here with my folks, years ago. I was hoping to give my kids a similar experience." She studied Kitty more closely. "In fact… I think we played together a few times when my family visited."

"Maybe." Kitty had played with most of the kids who came here as guests. It was no wonder she didn't remember every one. "Single mom?" Kitty asked. Which was nosy, but that was Kitty. Jake was curious, too. He'd noticed she didn't wear a wedding ring.

Summer hesitated, then nodded. "I guess…yeah, I'm a single mom," she said, her voice oddly flat. "I'll run up and change, and then…" She trailed off and walked toward her suite.

Watching her, Jake felt an unwelcome tug. He wasn't sure if it was sympathy for her situation or simple attraction.

Kitty looked thoughtfully from Summer to the kids. "She wanted to stay the week?"

"Yeah, and Dad told her it was okay last night, before I got home from the shop. How's he doing?"

Kitty just shook her head and went back into the kitchen. They were both worried about his increasing forgetfulness, not sure if it was something serious or just a byproduct of his grief. Mom had been gone six months, though, and Dad hadn't shown signs of improvement.

Summer came back downstairs in jeans and an old T-shirt. "Wow, that smells good," she said and then flashed a smile. "Don't worry, I'll keep my kids out of your hair while you have your Sunday dinner."

Jake had heard the kids saying they were hungry. "What are you going to eat?"

"Oh, I'll cook something on the camp stove. Or we'll just have sandwiches. I have a cooler in the van."

"That's ridiculous," Kitty said, wiping her hands as she came out of the kitchen. "Stay and eat with us."

Summer shook her head. "Thank you, that's kind, but you have your plans."

"No, I mean it," Kitty said. "Stay."

Summer's eyes widened. "For dinner, or for the week?"

The kids were running toward them. Jake and Kitty glanced at each other.

"Definitely for dinner," he said. "We'll discuss the week after we've all had something to eat."

As the kids dug into delicious fried chicken and mashed potatoes, Summer shot up a quick prayer of thanks. She'd asked God to help her provide, and here they were.

Now, she just had to convince Jake and Kitty to let her and her kids stay the week.

She prompted Rylee to wipe her mouth and helped her cut some chicken off the bone. She'd warned the kids to behave and use their manners, told them that it was very important. Rylee had just nodded, but Wyatt had picked up on her seriousness. "So they'll let us stay?"

"Well, yeah, but it's a grown-up decision. You just do your part, be the polite guy I know you can be, and we'll see."

Mr. Wright sat at one end of the table, Jake at the other. Kitty had taken the corner nearest the stove, and Wyatt was next to her. Summer and Rylee sat on the other side. Bowls and platters of food were in the middle of the table, family style. There seemed to be plenty left, even after the food had been passed around.

"This is great!" Wyatt said between bites. "May I have another piece?"

Kitty smiled as she passed the platter of chicken. "I like a kid who enjoys his food. My son is about your age and he's the same way. Growing like a weed."

They ate quietly for the most part, the only conversation praise for the food. Only Mr. Wright ate without enthusiasm, picking at his meal. Jake watched him and opened his mouth as if to speak, but Kitty shook her head, a quick "don't."

"So tell us about yourself," Jake said abruptly, looking at Summer.

She swallowed her food and silently reminded herself of what she intended to say. She'd crafted a response to just such a question before drifting off to sleep last night.

While Summer was collecting her thoughts, Rylee spoke up. "Our daddy went away," she said, "then we didn't have any money, so we came here."

Wyatt's mouth was full, but his cheeks turned pink. Summer's face heated, too. Both Kitty and Jake were looking at her, waiting for an explanation. Even Mr. Wright had looked up from his plate.

"It's true," she said, putting down her fork. "We have to move, but I wanted the kids to have a nice spring break first."

"Are you working?" Kitty asked quietly.

That was a complicated question. "I've been working part-time, at a craft store. But… I'll need to find a new job, something full-time."

She didn't elaborate on the worries that kept her up at night. Even full-time work, for someone like her without a degree, wouldn't pay for an apartment in the city, not in any kind of safe neighborhood. Let alone day care for Rylee.

"Sounds rough," Kitty said, her voice sympathetic.

Mr. Wright cleared his throat. "Have some more potatoes," he said, seeming to sense that Summer would appreciate a change of subject. He held out the bowl to Wyatt, who took a big scoop, and then held it to Rylee on the other side.

"Can you help me?" she asked shyly.

Summer started to reach for the bowl, but Mr. Wright was already spooning potatoes onto Rylee's plate. "There you go, little lady," he said. His voice sounded rusty, as if he didn't use it much.

Rylee smiled up at him. "Thank you. Are those ducks yours?"

Mr. Wright tilted his head to one side. "What ducks?"

"Down by the river," Wyatt explained.

"Those ducks? Ah, no. They belong to themselves, like all wild creatures." He smiled at Rylee. "But I'm sure glad they come to visit."

"Me, too," Rylee said.

Summer was glad they'd gotten off the subject of her husband and her finances. People looked at you differently when they knew you were practically penniless. She wanted to present herself as a stable person, a reliable, responsible guest.

"Can we feed the ducks?" Wyatt asked. "After lunch?"

"Well…" Mr. Wright's smile broadened. "Let me think about that." He was clearly enjoying drawing out the suspense.

Rylee's face went pink and her forehead creased. "I put my roll in my pocket for them," she confessed. She stood and reached into the pocket of her shorts, and pulled out a very smashed half of a roll.

"Rylee!" Summer frowned. "We need to ask, not take." Between Rylee pocketing food and Wyatt eating like he'd never had a meal before, her effort to seem reliable and stable was in jeopardy. "I'm sorry," she said to Jake and Kitty.

Wyatt was looking from Jake and Kitty to his mother. Suddenly, he stood and threw down his napkin. A roll bounced onto the floor. "I took one too. Guess we won't be allowed to stay." He stomped toward the door. "Nothing goes right," he added and then slammed the door.

Summer jumped up and hurried to the door. "Wyatt. You stay where you can see the house."

"I will," he grumped, and marched toward the river, tension and anger in every step. Summer watched him for a moment, then returned to the table.

"I wanna stay." Rylee's eyes filled with tears. "I'm sorry I took the roll."

"Well, now, I don't see why you can't stay," Mr. Wright said.

"Really?" Rylee's eyes widened as she looked at the older man.

"Really." He patted her hand, then fixed Kitty and Jake with a stern gaze. "Mama and I were always about hospitality. Things have changed, but we don't have to kick out a real nice lady and her kids."

Jake and Kitty exchanged glances.

"I'll work on cleaning up the place, as a way to help and pay for our keep," Summer said. "There's plenty of work for a week."

"A month or more," Kitty said. "This place is big-time dirty."

She seemed to be on board. Jake was the holdout, but she sensed he carried a lot of power in the family. "I can pay instead, the rate that was on the website," she said quickly.

It was what she'd planned to do, even though it had cut into her miniscule savings account.

"Cleaning is worth more," Kitty said. "We should pay you."

"We don't know if we even want to open the place up," Jake said. "There's no point in getting it cleaned up if we're just going to stay closed."

"Even if you want to sell it," Summer said desperately, "you'll want it looking good. I can make that happen."

"My son's off, too, this coming week," Kitty said slowly. "He'd enjoy some new playmates. We live right next door," she added, looking at Summer.

"Then we can stay the week?" Summer's heart rose. Wyatt would be so happy.

"I said you could," Mr. Wright said.

"Okay by me," Kitty said. "One mom to another, I feel for you."

They all looked at Jake. "If she passes a background check," he said.

"Jake!" Kitty gave him a fake whack on the arm. "That's rude. Mom and Dad never did background checks on guests."

"We don't know her from anyone," Jake said stubbornly.

"He has trust issues," Kitty said to Summer. "But unless he turns up a prison sentence or finds out that you're running from the law, you can stay."

Relief coursed through Summer and she sent up a quick prayer of thanks. God was providing. Maybe just a week at a time, but she was grateful. "I'll work hard," she promised.

"I'll help," Rylee piped up.

Mr. Wright smiled at her. "Right now, you can come help me feed those ducks," he said.

"Okay!" She slid out of her chair and hugged him. "I'm

gonna tell Wyatt we can stay!" She rushed out the back door. Mr. Wright followed her, chuckling.

"I'm sorry," Summer said to the brother and sister. "They usually have better manners. Well, sometimes," she amended. She stood and carried her plate to the sink, then returned for the serving dishes.

Kitty rose and carried over her dish. "Let me clean up," Summer told the woman. "You cooked."

"Sounds fine to me," Kitty said. "I have no problem napping on the couch."

Jake stood, picked up his own dish and his father's. "I'll help," he said without a trace of a smile, "and we'll talk."

Summer's stomach turned over. There was another barrier to get through before her kids could have the spring break of their dreams. A handsome, grouchy barrier named Jake.

Chapter Three

Jake carried dishes to the counter. Summer had already taken up her position at the sink and was rinsing plates and loading them into the dishwasher.

The kitchen was a mess, with dirty pans and bowls and crumbs all over the counters. Typical of when Kitty cooked, but that was fine with Jake. A mess meant he'd have more time to interrogate Summer and try to figure out whether she was who she said she was.

Sun slanted through the kitchen window, casting light on her face and making her hair shine. She was young, definitely under thirty, and yet she had two kids including a ten-year-old. She'd started young, being a mom.

He brought in the last of the dishes and then took a sponge and wiped down the table, thinking.

He didn't want to be a jerk. Didn't want to lack Christian charity. But he had to protect his father. He hadn't protected his wife, and she had paid the price, along with their unborn child. And sure, she'd been at fault in the accident, technically, but he'd been the one who'd sent her off on an emotional tear that had resulted in way too much drinking and a fatal crash with a tree.

Dad was vulnerable now, since Mom's death. He didn't always shower, didn't always shave, definitely didn't keep his quarters clean. He was depressed in a classical sense. His doctor had said as much and recommended medication, but Dad had refused to take it. The doctor had understood, and had told them about studies saying exercise was as effective as medication for treating depression. The issue was, Dad didn't want to go to a gym or out for a jog. He'd always gotten exercise naturally, working on cars for a living, and keeping up the guesthouse in his time off, gardening and repairing things.

Now, he rarely came into the shop and he had let the guesthouse grounds go. Kitty came in and cleaned Dad's room every couple of weeks, and Jake was responsible for the kitchen and living areas. Obviously, he'd been slacking off on his duties. He looked ruefully around the kitchen, noticing the stacks of mail, containers of food that should have been put away, books that needed to be returned to the library.

The floor shone, though, and that was Summer's doing. Having her live in for a week and make the rest of the place shine would take a load off his mind. Unless she turned out to be a crook who was out to steal from Dad. Like that Hortense woman who'd befriended Dad in the weeks after Mom's funeral and had gotten him to loan her several thousand dollars before skipping town. Jake's blood boiled just thinking about it.

He leaned on the counter beside Summer. "So what's your real story?"

Her hands stilled on the pan she was washing. "It's like Rylee said. The children's father left and we're short on funds."

"No divorce settlement? Child support?"

She scrubbed harder at the pan. The lemony smell of dish soap joined with the floral scent of her hair, a pleasing combination. The pan clanked as she set it in the drainer. Finally, she looked at him. "He has another family."

"What?" He grabbed a dish towel and dried the pan she'd washed.

She scrubbed at another pot. "Turns out he was married to someone else the whole time we were married. He has a wife and kids over in Ohio."

"You didn't know?" He'd heard of that type of thing happening, probably in some TV docudrama, but he'd never known a victim of it.

"Not until six months ago. He traveled a lot for work." She glanced over at him. "I was stupid. I should have been checking his credit card statements and going through his phone, but it didn't occur to me. I'm not really the type."

"So... Where does that leave you?"

She sighed. "Most of our money and property was in his name, and since our marriage is considered void, I'm not entitled to any of it."

"Child support?"

She nodded. "He's been sending me money, but it's not enough to live on." Her cheeks were pink. "Look, I don't know you. I wouldn't be sharing all this except that I'm hoping you'll let me stay here and work for the week."

"Why are you just looking for a week's work, if you're in that situation?"

She handed over the pot she'd been washing and went at the utensils. "I was hoping for more hours at the craft store where I've worked for years," she said. "Hoping for a promotion to manager, but when I met with my boss to ask, it didn't go well."

"Why's that?" He watched her for signs of lying. Had she been robbing the till?

"He told me what it would take to become a manager, and

it wasn't…acceptable. Wasn't a price I was willing to pay." A muscle tensed in her jaw.

Jake frowned. "If you're saying what I think you're saying, that's sexual harassment and you should report it. Get a lawyer and take him to court."

She turned off the water, faced him and planted her hands on her hips. "I *know* it's sexual harassment. I may report it, but at the moment, until I find something else, I need the paycheck. Plus, I have enough legal problems, and fees, on my hands already."

He studied her face and saw no deception there. Unwillingly, a sense of protectiveness for her rose in him.

"I can give you references from a coworker at the craft store, and from a couple of people I clean for on the side," she went on. "From my pastor, if that would help. Not from my manager, though. He's a little angry I didn't fall in with his proposal when he made it."

"Which was when?"

"Last week." She sighed. "I wouldn't be surprised if he found some reason to fire me. Which, yes, I could do a lawsuit for that, too. I know. I'm just busy trying to survive at the moment."

He considered what she'd said. She'd painted a picture of desperation and betrayal, and he felt for her. "It sounds like you need a whole new job, not just a week's work."

She drew in a breath and let it out slowly. It made him realize that this was hard for her, being interrogated by a stranger. That he was trying her patience. But to her credit, she kept going. "I do need longer term work. I scour the job sites every night after the kids go to bed. But after giving up our house, I just really needed to get away, and the kids did, too." She sighed and looked up at him, her eyes vulnerable.

"I'm not always the most practical, as you can probably tell, but I'm trying to learn to be."

Happy shouts from outside made them both look out the window. His father was smiling, watching the children throwing bread to the ducks, who were starting to boldly come onshore.

"They don't have a grandpa," Summer said, sounding wistful. "And now, they don't have much of a father. They're hungry for attention from a good man."

Jake nodded. "It might be good for my dad to have a couple more kids around, too. He's pretty depressed."

"So can we stay the week, if I provide you with references that check out? I'll get the place into good shape, and that might help with your dad's depression, too."

The sun glinted on her hair, and he caught a whiff of flowery perfume. Again, he felt a jolt of attraction.

He stifled it immediately. He'd made a firm decision to stay away from women after what he'd done. This was the first time he'd felt any inkling of wanting to break that vow.

But he guessed he could handle Summer's presence for a week. He'd keep busy. The Lord knew, there was plenty to catch up on at the shop.

"You can stay," he said, "if your references check out."

"Thank you!" For a minute, he thought she was going to hug him, but she just smiled broadly and started looking around the kitchen. "I really appreciate it, and I promise you, we'll leave things better than they were. Hopefully including your dad. If it's okay with you, I'll start with tidying up and cleaning in here. Oh and..." She pulled out her phone. "If you have a note pad, I'll give you the names and numbers of my references."

He felt good that he'd put the happiness back in her face. It seemed like that was her natural mood, and to have restored that to her, even temporarily, lifted his spirits.

He just needed to make sure he didn't get too carried away with liking to make her feel good. Nor with protecting her and her sweet kids. That was a type of temptation he was determined to resist.

On Wednesday evening, in the parking lot of the big box store, Summer and the kids helped Jake load bags into the bed of his truck. They climbed in. As Jake drove them back toward the guesthouse, Summer's mind shifted into higher gear.

She worked hard so far this week, hard enough that she'd used up most of the guesthouse's cleaning supplies. Hence this trip with Jake to purchase more. He'd said he wanted to buy something for the shop, and she'd needed a few things for the kids, which she'd gotten. It was a help to ride with him, since her van was unreliable. At least according to Jake. He'd looked at it and made enough repairs that it could be driven, but he'd said it really needed a full overhaul.

She couldn't afford what that would cost, and she hated to put it on a credit card, but she'd probably have to. She hoped the van would make it back to the city.

The kids were enjoying their spring break, which was the main thing. They'd had good weather, and two of the three days, Kitty's son, Mason, had come over. He and Wyatt had hit it off right away.

Wyatt and Rylee were rosy and even a little suntanned, and were sleeping soundly each night. They were both more relaxed, and Summer felt pleased that the break was working out as she'd hoped.

Now, though, she was thinking longer term and wondering

what to do. She was already dreading the thought of going back to town and her job.

As they approached the small downtown of River Haven, she noticed lights on in the little library. "Do you mind dropping us off here?" she asked Jake. "We'll walk back to the guesthouse."

"Library!" Rylee bounced in the booster seat they'd moved from the van into Jake's truck.

"Can I just play outside?" Wyatt asked. He was a reluctant reader, preferring active play.

"No, but I'm sure they have car books you can look at," she said, and he grudgingly agreed.

"Not a problem," Jake said, slowing down. "I need to stop by myself. Dad's out of books, and I could use something new to read too."

Great. More time being watched by Jake.

He'd been perfectly nice, and in fact, he'd told her they were going to pay her for her time in addition to letting them stay the week free. But he was definitely keeping an eye on her when he wasn't working next door, and she was way too conscious of his dark, brooding gaze.

His presence made her uncomfortable, and no wonder. Guys were trouble, as evidenced by her so-called husband and her boss.

Jake parked and they walked inside.

The library was a small, squat building, unassuming on the outside. Inside, one large room held adult books. A display of spring cleaning books and another of craft books flanked the circulation desk, where an aide was working at a computer. Several people browsed the shelves, a couple of them waving at Jake.

From an adjoining room came the sound of kids' voices, and she guided Wyatt and Rylee toward them. It looked like they'd happened upon a kids' story time. A group of six or seven preschoolers sat in a circle in front of an enthusiastic-looking woman who was reading a colorful picture book. Rylee immediately found a carpet square and sat down.

Wyatt looked grouchy, but when Summer found him a section of kids' books about cars, he was at least mildly interested. "You stay here and look at the books, and keep an eye on Rylee," she ordered him. "I'll be right out there if you need me." She gestured toward a cluster of tables in the adult room.

She found the career section and pulled out several promising-looking books, two about résumés and one about finding your dream job. She opened the first résumé book and started skimming.

It didn't take long for her worries to escalate. She had so little to offer. Years of retail experience, plus cleaning houses. No education beyond high school and a couple of community college classes.

How was she going to support herself and her kids?

She'd been so impractical, so gullible. She'd gone merrily along, taking care of her kids and home, doing jobs she enjoyed, but that didn't pay well. She'd expected her marriage to last, even though there had been plenty of signs that things were deteriorating. Why hadn't she paid more attention, listened to her intuition?

Chuck had spent so much time on the road, and she'd wondered, occasionally, whether he was faithful. But when he'd come home, he'd always seemed glad to see her and the kids. That had changed the past two years, when he'd seemed more volatile and unhappy. Their marriage had been cooling off to the point where she'd been pretty lonely, except that a mom rarely had time to be lonely.

And then she'd gotten the visit that had destroyed her illusions, from Wyatt's other wife.

She closed the résumé book and opened the dream job one. Just as she started to read, Jake came and sat across from her. "What would it be?" he asked.

She frowned, puzzled.

"Your dream job," he clarified. "What would it be?"

She *had* thought about that, a little, before she'd become desperate. "Something crafty or artsy. Decorating, maybe. Or party planning, event planning. But I don't have the credentials. What's yours?"

He smiled. "I'm doing it. I love working on cars, helping people get back on the road. I like living where I grew up, near my dad and sister. I'm a pretty simple guy."

"That's nice," she said, meaning it. She never met men like that, who were just comfortable with who they were and what they did. So many people these days seemed unhappy, always striving for more.

A sudden shout from the kids' area brought her to her feet. "That's Wyatt," she said, and rushed toward the loud, disruptive voices.

Wyatt and another boy were yelling at one another. As Summer reached them, another mom came hurrying over.

"What's going on?" Summer put a hand on Wyatt's shoulder, to calm him and to be ready to hold him back if things got physical.

The other boy looked up at his mother. "All I did was ask if his dad was gonna help him build an engine," he said.

"My dad's not here!" Wyatt yelled the words, his face red.

The kid shrugged, his expression puzzled. "I thought that was your dad," he said, pointing at Jake, who'd walked toward them and was standing a distance away. "He works at the car repair place we go to."

"No, hon, that's Mr. Wright," the other mom said. "His wife…he doesn't have a wife and kids."

At the sight of Wyatt's pushed-out lower lip, as Summer realized what had upset him, sympathy washed over her. "That boy just made a mistake," she said to Wyatt. "He doesn't know anything about your dad."

Wyatt looked at the kid, his eyes narrow, and then his shoulders relaxed. "Sorry," he mumbled.

"It's okay." The kid turned away and knelt down beside a book the boys had apparently been looking at together, a heavily illustrated volume about motors.

"I'm sorry," Summer said to the mom. "We've gone through some tough transitions lately, but that's no excuse for yelling."

"I said I'm sorry." Wyatt's frown deepened.

The other mom shrugged. "Kids will be kids. No big deal. Come on, Josiah, it's time to go home."

Summer steered Wyatt to a quiet corner of the children's area. "Want to talk about what just happened?"

Wyatt stared at the floor. "I thought he was teasing me like the kids at school."

Summer's heart rate quickened. "You were getting teased at school?"

"About Dad," he said, his voice low.

Summer's heart ached. She'd hoped that Chuck's double life wouldn't become known. She gave Wyatt a quick hug. "I'm sorry that's been happening. You should have told me."

He looked up from the floor. "I don't wanna go back," he said.

Summer sucked in a breath and let it out in a sigh. "I understand," she said. And she did, now, better than before. "I think we have to, but let's enjoy our week here for now."

She had to find a way to make things better for her kids. Not just for spring break, but for real life.

That night, after the kids were asleep, she texted her friend Marti, a teacher in Wyatt's school, to find out more about the teasing. Her friend called immediately. "Word about what happened to you has gotten around," Marti said. "A lot of the teachers know, and I'd guess some of the parents, too. I wouldn't think they'd talk about it in front of their kids, but some parents are just careless. Or mean. Gosh, I'm sorry that's been happening."

"Me, too," Summer said. "You haven't heard anything about Wyatt getting into trouble or having conflicts with other kids, have you?"

Her friend hesitated. "I did hear there was some teasing and arguing going on in Wyatt's class," she said. "I don't know if he was involved, but maybe you should talk to his teacher."

"Maybe I will," Summer said, but after she'd hung up, she wondered.

As a mother, she wanted to protect her son from teasing. But she also knew that those kinds of adult efforts were often ineffective. Kids would be kids, like the mom at the library had said, and a parent couldn't expect to intervene in every conflict. At some point, children had to work it out between themselves. If Wyatt had reacted badly to the teasing, it had probably intensified. She needed to talk to him about how to handle any teasing he experienced.

She'd been thinking a lot about her future and what to do next. To help figure that out, she messaged one of her coworkers, the one who'd given her a good reference. "I've been meaning to call you," the woman said. "Mr. Jenkins overheard me giving the reference, and he asked if you were working somewhere else. I told him it was temporary, but he's started asking everyone about your work. He's looking for dirt on you."

After Summer turned off her phone for the night, she lay in bed and tried to sleep. But her thoughts were whirling.

If she lost her job…well, she'd wanted to quit, anyway, after what had happened. She needed more hours and more pay. But it wasn't going to be easy to find something, not with her lack of credentials.

She spent a little time looking through her Bible and praying over the encouraging verses she'd been highlighting lately. That helped, but she still couldn't sleep.

Finally, she got up and dressed and went downstairs. No point in lying around wakeful when there was work to be done.

She filled a bucket with cleaning supplies and went into the room they called the reading room. A fireplace, a couple of big wing chairs and a table with a chessboard gave it the feel of an old English library in a manor house. Without turning on any lights, she walked over to the big window.

Moonlight shone on the river, making a silvery, rippling mirror. Still-bare branches crisscrossed over it. A deer emerged from the trees, and then another.

Summer's heart seized up at the beauty of it. When you compared these surroundings to those they'd had in the city, there was no contest. No question of where she wanted to be, where she wanted her kids to be.

Was she just avoiding reality? Back in the city, she'd face her manager. She'd have to deal with his making moves on her, and his anger when she resisted him. That wasn't workable. She'd have to find another job, and she'd also need to locate a place to live that wasn't too expensive.

Just like Wyatt, she didn't want to go back.

Even more than not wanting to go back herself, she didn't want to send Wyatt back into an environment of gossip and possible bullying. Hopefully, their domestic drama would be forgotten by the time Rylee got a little older, but you never knew. People who'd known the four of them as a family might always find their troubles a little too interesting.

Chuck had piled more pain on them than he knew. And she felt Wyatt's pain as if it were her own. Her heart ached, just thinking of his hurt, angry face.

Wyatt was happy here, fishing with Mr. Wright and playing with kids who didn't know his background. She wanted with everything in her to keep that smile on his face.

But to stay here, she would have to find work that paid the bills and an affordable place to live. While housing was cheaper here, no doubt, there was less of it. And the selection of decently paying jobs would be miniscule.

She straightened up and selected a soft cloth from her supply bucket. She sprayed it with cleaning spray and started wiping down surfaces.

There were no perfect options or answers. Going back to Pittsburgh would be rough, but staying here didn't seem possible.

Father, she prayed, *help me figure out what to do.* Rhythmically she dusted, repeating the prayer inside her head: *show me what to do, show me what to do.*

When she dusted the windowsill, she looked out and saw a small, cupped birds' nest, illuminated in the moonlight. Inside were two blue eggs.

And then the moon disappeared behind a cloud, and she could no longer see the nest.

Build a nest, here. The thought came to her clearly.

Could she do it? Could she and the kids settle down here?

It was only possible, she realized, if she could combine rent with work, as she had this week.

So there was her answer. She'd try to talk Jake and Mr. Wright into letting her little family stay. She just had to come up with a plan that would be irresistible to the two men. And there was no time like the present to get started.

Chapter Four

"Do you want to come with me to the shop?" Jake asked Wyatt at breakfast.

He'd noticed that Wyatt was interested in cars and motors, had seen the books Wyatt had been looking at in the library.

Since the little family would be leaving soon, Jake had decided to try to give the boy a good memory to take with him. Maybe even a thought of a future career.

"Can I, Mom?" Wyatt's eyes were shining. "Please?"

"If you do just what Mr. Jake says and don't get in the way, yes." She looked at Jake. "Thank you. That's a very kind thing to do."

And there it was, the other reason he'd wanted to help Wyatt out. His beautiful mother. Jake's gaze met hers. It was hard to look away.

Uh-oh. If he wasn't careful, he'd get too attached to making her happy.

Long term, you can't, he reminded himself. *You're a rotten husband.*

Jake enjoyed the day more than he'd expected. Wyatt loved looking around the shop and asked intelligent questions. He knew more than Jake would've expected of a kid who didn't grow up in the trade. When Jake let Wyatt get under a car, the kid's expression was priceless.

At the end of the day, Wyatt rushed into the house ahead of Jake, yelling, "Mom, Mom!" He proceeded to tell his mother the story of his day in the kind of excruciating detail only a ten-year-old boy could manage.

Jake was impressed that Summer listened attentively.

After Wyatt had run upstairs to wash up and help his sister do the same, Summer turned to Jake. For a minute, he thought she was going to hug him. For a minute, he thought he wanted her to. But she just gripped his hand with both of hers. "Thank you. This day meant so much to him, and to me, too. More than you can ever imagine."

"He's a good kid," Jake said gruffly.

She gave him a funny look, and that was when he realized he was holding onto her hands. They felt small inside his, small but calloused. She was a working woman.

Her hair smelled like raspberries in the summer sun. Her eyes glowed, so pretty. He didn't want to let go of her; he wanted to pull her closer.

Trying to get ahold of himself, he dropped her hands, looked away and caught a glimpse of the clock on the wall. It had been a wedding gift to Jake and his wife, something about all our tomorrows.

There hadn't been enough tomorrows, and even fewer happy ones, for his wife. When she'd died, he'd vowed he'd not subject another woman to the dangers and risks of himself as a husband.

Yet here he was, getting all misty-eyed over not only Summer, but her child. Children, because Rylee was a little cutie, too, just coming into her own.

His own child hadn't even had a chance to be born. She'd been killed in the crash that had killed her mother. A crash caused by him, and so what was he doing, dreaming of a happy future with this nice little family?

He turned away. "I've got plans for dinner," he said gruffly. "Dad and me both. Make yourself at home in the kitchen." He walked out of the room before he could spend any more time admiring her pretty face.

It turned out that the children were invited to Jake's sister's place for dinner. Kitty called and invited Summer, too. But she declined, explaining that she needed to do some things and thanking Kitty effusively for keeping the kids busy and happy.

Once she had the guesthouse to herself, she thought hard.

The day had been wonderful for Wyatt. All that male attention, and in a subject area he loved. That was something he'd needed to get from his father, but the opportunity had never arisen. Besides, Chuck hadn't liked working with his hands.

Wyatt had never excelled in school, but he loved to build things and fix things. All on his own, he'd taken apart an old alarm clock to see how it worked and had put it back together. He'd fixed the toaster when it had given out in the middle of breakfast. And he was always watching videos and looking at magazines about cars.

The idea of staying here, in this very place where maybe Wyatt could get a little more experience in the auto shop next door, had become even more appealing. But for some reason, this afternoon, Jake had closed down and withdrawn. She sensed it would take some persuasion to show him that she could do something for him, help him get the inn running again, give his father something to look forward to and bring life into the guesthouse again.

This afternoon, she and Rylee had discovered several boxes full of Easter decorations in the storage closet across from their suite. Since holidays were the inn's trademark, she decided to get the decorations out and decorate the place for Easter. Not a lot, since the holiday was only a few days away, but just enough to show the men what she could do if given the opportunity.

She brought two big boxes down from the storage closet, staggering under their weight. She set them down in the kitchen and opened them up.

One, she saw immediately, was outdoor decorations. Wreaths and hanging eggs and a big white rabbit that would look cute beside the door. She put up a wreath on each door that faced the street and hung colorful eggs on the two small trees beside the office.

She went back inside and opened the box labeled Kitchen—Easter. It held a different theme. Not secular Easter, with its bunnies and eggs and pretty pastels, but the true meaning of the holiday.

She pulled out a large, plain cross with a small framed verse attached to the bottom. "I am the resurrection and the life," it read, with *John 11:25* beneath.

She held it and let the words refocus her: away from her problems with Chuck and her boss, away from her worries, and onto Christ, who'd sacrificed His life to cancel her sins and those of all believers.

A rough-hewn wooden plaque held Jesus's stark last words from Luke 23:34: "Father, forgive them, for they know not what they do."

His last breath had been a request that hateful people be forgiven.

Christians were tasked with trying to live like Christ. Summer wasn't anywhere near forgiving Chuck for what he'd done, but she could see, suddenly, that it was a goal to strive for.

She needed to ask forgiveness for herself, too. She'd made

plenty of mistakes, chief among them that she hadn't been a watchful enough guardian of her kids. She hadn't seen the danger coming, from within or without. She hadn't prepared carefully, so that she'd be ready to pick up full support of her kids financially when Chuck had proved unreliable.

But Christ had died for everyone's sins, and that meant that despite her mistakes, she could live free.

The conventional idea of sins was the big ones, theft and greed and lust. Well, she'd been pretty good about those. But there were other sins, like not living up to one's potential or planning ahead and taking care of one's own. There, she was a true sinner.

She was working hard to fix all that, and worrying plenty, but she needed to remember that God had it in control. She had to keep working—she started unwrapping more beautiful crosses and ceramic scenes—but she didn't have to worry. It was all in God's hands.

She finished the decorations, humming. She was just straightening the last sculpture, an empty, purple-draped cross with the words *He is Risen* beneath, when she heard the car outside. Jake and Mr. Wright were returning, and she felt a twinge of panic. Would they like what she'd done?

Mr. Wright walked in, looked around, and his greeting died on his lips. His eyes shone with unshed tears as he walked around the kitchen, touching each decoration.

Had it been a mistake? She walked over and, hesitantly, put an arm around the older man. "I'm sorry if this makes you sad," she said. "I thought it would be nice to decorate, but maybe I was wrong."

"Oh, don't be sorry, little lady," he said. "This is what Mama would have wanted. She loved to decorate. Loved how happy it made people."

"I remember," Summer said. "Especially one Christmas

when we came, after my grandparents died. Mom was really sad, but your wife was so kind and this place was so warm and festive. You and your wife helped us have a good Christmas despite the sadness."

"That's what she wanted this to be," he said. "A place where families, or just lonely people, could come for the holidays. Where they could feel festive and happy, and be among friends, old and new." He paused. "I've let that go, and I shouldn't have."

She was pretty sure she could present her proposal to Mr. Wright this minute, and he'd accept and hire her.

But he wasn't the only one she needed to convince. Jake was more the decision-maker. And he was coming into the kitchen right now, a frown on his face.

When he opened his mouth, she braced herself for an attack. But before Jake could speak, Mr. Wright looked at his son, eyes shining. "It's just how your mother used to decorate," he said. "It's wonderful, isn't it?"

Through the open screen door, Summer could hear her kids' voices. They'd be coming inside any minute. It was now or never. She faced the two men. "I could make it happen again," she said. "I could make the guesthouse shine, build up the business and manage it for you. Decorate for every holiday and set up activities, just like before. Would you consider hiring me longer term?"

Then she held her breath. What would they say?

Jake looked from beautiful, dangerous Summer, to his father, to the doorway through which her kids were about to come, decorated with Mom's favorite springtime wreath.

He could see that his father loved the idea. Dad had perked up since Summer and her kids had arrived. Not like he used to be, but Jake could see the potential. Dad was much more energetic than he'd been even a week ago.

But for Jake, the potential for disaster was just too big. Even now, looking at Summer's pretty, expectant face, he felt the urge to pull her into his arms, to protect her from the dangers of the world, to try to do a better job than he had before. To be a good influence on those cute kids of hers.

But he wasn't able to do that. He'd been tested and he'd failed the test. Now, with Summer, the stakes were higher because there were a couple of very sweet kids involved. "We can't hire you," he said abruptly.

"Why not, son?" His father frowned. "Would your mother want us living in a cave like this, when there are people who need what Holiday Haven has to offer?"

Jake crossed his arms and leaned back against the counter. "We haven't even decided whether to reopen the guesthouse. It would be work, a lot of it. We'd need a cleaning staff and an event planner and a decorator, just for starters. I'm too busy keeping the shop afloat to be able to do all that."

"Your mother fulfilled all those roles herself," Dad said.

"And I could do the same," Summer broke in. "With advice and help, of course, but I could get that from the two of you."

The kids burst in. "We had a blast, Mom!" Wyatt yelled. Then he went serious. "But Rylee's tired. She fell asleep when we were watching the movie, and Mrs. MacIntyre is bringing her in."

He held the screen door open, and Kitty came in with Rylee asleep on one shoulder. She handed Rylee over to Summer. "I need to get back to Mason." She waved away Summer's thanks and hurried out the door. "Nice decorations," she called back to them.

Summer held Rylee against her shoulder. "I'll leave you

men to think about my offer," she said quietly. "Come on, Wyatt. Time to get ready for bed."

Jake watched her go, his heart tugging back and forth. Tugging toward her, and then pulling back into his chest, hiding, troubled.

"I say we take her up on her offer," Dad said.

Jake shook his head. "I don't think it's wise. We need to think it through, at least."

Dad waved a hand. "I've thought. I feel better than I have since your mother died, and it's because I'm doing something, not just hiding out. Your mother wouldn't want me to just wither and die. It's the season of new life, and I feel it."

"But… I just don't think—"

"What are you so afraid of?" his father demanded.

No way could he admit the truth: that he was afraid he wouldn't be able to resist Summer, that she'd somehow fall in with his plans and care back. That the kids would too, and that he'd then ruin their lives the way he'd ruined his wife and unborn child's.

But was he really such a wimp that he couldn't be in the house with a beautiful woman without giving in to his feelings?

"You're afraid," Dad said. "Afraid of coming out of that shop. Afraid of having this place full of life and happiness again."

"I'm not," he defended automatically.

Dad ignored him and plowed on. "Ever since Amanda died, you've been working all the time. Hiding away from people and getting grouchier by the day. Which, to be fair, I've been doing too. But Easter seems like a good time for us to get out of ourselves and try to do a little more with our lives."

"Are you really up for that?" He studied his father. "Just

a week ago, you weren't even showering and shaving every day. How do you know you're not going to sink back into that again? If you do, you won't want a bunch of strangers going through the house having needs and demands."

"Do you think I'm too old to change?" Dad asked, frowning up at him. "I may be seventy years old, but there's life in me yet. I still have more to give. This little family has made me realize that. And here Summer's offering us a way to start contributing. Offering to take Mom's place, carry on her traditions." Dad pointed at the sky. "That's from God. You know your mother would say it. Maybe it's from her, whispering in the Lord's ear."

Jake blew out a breath. His father clearly wanted this. Jake was cautious, worried. He didn't want to open the place and then have it all be too much. What if Summer did the job for a few months and then quit, dumping it all on them?

But looking into his father's eyes, Jake couldn't tamp down the flame there. It was too new, too fragile. "I guess we can give it a try," he said.

Chapter Five

On Saturday morning, Jake and his father headed to River Haven's annual Easter Egg hunt along with most of the rest of the townspeople. This year, Summer and her kids walked along beside them.

The sight of the inflatable Easter eggs, flat metal bunnies as tall as a child, and yard signs with slogans like Happy Easter, Peeps made Jake remember last year. They'd driven Mom down and watched from the car as the kids, Mason included, ran through the park hunting for eggs, then visited the Easter bunny.

Now, Mom was gone.

Jake hadn't expected to go this year, hadn't really thought about it. But everything had changed when Summer and her kids had moved in. She'd heard about the event from Kitty, and so had her kids. The kids couldn't stop talking about it, and Dad had chimed in with stories, and somehow, they were all attending together.

As they approached River Haven's downtown, the sound of a band filled the air, playing jolly kids' tunes. An emcee broke in, telling everyone the Easter Egg hunt would start in half an hour.

The River Runs Through It Coffee Shop had set up a stand selling coffee and cinnamon rolls and fruit cups. Those who wanted more substantial fare could get it from The Hungry Hubcap, a former gas station now made into a restaurant and serving a little of everything, including hearty breakfasts.

Kids ran around the park, pulled back by their parents from the egg hunt area. It was a nice day, brisk and sunny, and the park was crowded.

Jake kept an eye on his dad, who'd basically been a hermit for the past six months. He'd brought his cane and was walking well, but he looked a little overwhelmed by the noise and the people.

Rylee had run ahead with Wyatt, but she circled back, looked up at Jake's dad and took his hand.

Dad looked down at her and smiled.

Jake's heart tugged. His dad would have loved to have a granddaughter. Mom would've, too. And they might have, if Jake hadn't fought by phone with his wife and sent her rushing away to her death in a one-car drunk driving accident.

He felt uneasy about his father getting close to Summer and her kids, not feeling sure of whether he could trust them and whether they'd stay around.

"I remember doing the Easter Egg hunt as a kid." Summer swung into step beside him.

"You were here for Easter?" Jake asked.

"A couple of times. Mom and Dad enjoyed spending holidays here. They started coming right before I was born. There was a picture of me with the Easter Bunny right here in this park, when I was a baby."

"You came when you were older, too?" Jake saw two kids on bikes approaching them, jabbering together, not watching where they were going. He took Summer's arm and tugged her out of their path. "Careful, kids," he said. He must have spoken sternly, because they looked at him, wide-eyed, and slowed way down.

Summer's slender arm felt good to hold. He didn't want to let go, but he forced himself to do so.

Summer didn't seem affected in the same way. "We came at least once a year, up until I was nine or ten," she said. "After that, we were living more out West and didn't get back as often."

"Should we remember each other?"

"I have a few memories of a cute teenage boy running around." Her cheeks went pink. "But just vague ones. After all, you're *so* much older than I am." She lifted an eyebrow and smiled.

She was teasing him. "Older and wiser," he said.

"Are you, though?"

"Not really." He looked down at her. Tried to keep from smiling. Couldn't.

"There you are." Kitty approached with her son, Mason. She glanced from Summer to Jake and tilted her head to one side.

Jake ignored his sister's meaningful look and ruffled his nine-year-old's nephew's hair. "Ready to get the most eggs?" he asked Mason.

"Yeah!" Mason said.

Wyatt ran back to join their group.

"Are you ten?" Mason demanded.

Wyatt nodded.

"Then we're in the same group. Nine and ten-year-olds. We should make a plan to get the most eggs."

"Yeah!" Wyatt said. "Let's scope it out." The two boys went off toward the corral where kids were waiting for their age groups to be called.

"You and Rylee had better get up there," Kitty told Summer. "Parents are allowed to go in with the under-fives. They're about to start."

"Let's go, Rylee!" Summer and Rylee raced toward the corral. Identical dark hair shone.

"She's pretty," Kitty said in a low voice.

"Who?" Jake asked, although he knew. He looked around and saw that they were alone. Wyatt and Mason had joined the other kids in the waiting area, and Dad had stopped to talk to a friend.

"Summer. I saw how you looked at her."

"You saw wrong. Nothing's going to happen between us."

"Because…"

"Too much else on my plate," Jake said. "Let's go up and watch the kids." He wasn't about to discuss his no-women resolution with Kitty. She would only try to talk him out of it.

Which would be pointless. There was no way he'd get together with Summer. Not when he'd botched his marriage. He wasn't good at relationships, and no way was he going to inflict himself on someone who already had struggles on her hands, like Summer did.

They went over and stood near the boys, who were talking with some other kids about a community baseball league that was starting up. "You gonna play?" Mason asked Wyatt.

"I might," Wyatt said, but he looked uneasy. "I don't know if we're sticking around."

And then the gates opened and the little kids and their parents rushed out, finding the barely hidden eggs and putting them into little paper baskets. There were shrieks and a few tears. Rylee ran around looking thrilled. Summer watched and encouraged her.

"You should take pictures," Kitty urged him. "I would, but I forgot my phone. Go on, take a few pictures to send to her. This is a moment and a memory, and single moms don't get that many pictures of themselves doing fun things."

She was right, and it was no hardship to zoom in on

Summer and Rylee and take a few shots. He caught one of Summer laughing, her dark hair flying behind her, and was tempted to study it too long. He put his phone away and glanced at his sister's pensive face. Kitty was a single mom, too. He resolved to take more pictures of her and Mason together.

Soon the little kids' hunt was over, and after an interlude for the six-to-eight-year-olds, Wyatt and Mason's turn came. They rushed out and ran around, searching for the harder-to-find eggs.

Summer and Rylee came over and showed them her Easter basket containing four eggs. "I found more," Rylee explained, "but you can only take as many as how old you are."

"Aimee Christianson didn't get that memo," murmured Kitty, nodding toward a woman they both knew, who was loading lots of eggs from her toddler's basket into her purse.

The noise from the egg hunt got louder, and they all cheered for Wyatt and Mason.

Summer knelt beside Rylee. "After this, we'll go see the Easter Bunny," she said, pointing in the direction of the guy in the white bunny suit.

"I'm scared," Rylee said.

Dad had come over and heard Rylee's words. "He looks scary, but he's really just a man in a bunny suit. Friend of mine, actually. And he has candy."

"He *does?"* Rylee sounded amazed.

"Yep. But it's up to you. I can probably get you a little candy if you don't want to talk to him."

"It's okay either way, honey," Summer said. "The Easter Bunny's bringing you candy tomorrow." Her hand flew to her mouth and she looked stricken.

"Forgot something?" Kitty asked, looking amused.

"Easter baskets," she mouthed.

"I have some shopping to do, too," Kitty said. "There are a couple of stores in town that would have what you're looking for. I'm sure Dad and Jake would take the kids to see the EB while we shop a little."

"Oh, I couldn't—" Summer started, and then stopped, looking at Rylee.

The little girl was standing beside Dad, listening while he explained that the Easter Bunny couldn't hurt her and was very nice.

Wyatt and Mason came rushing out, red-faced and sweating, crowing over their finds. The kids all knelt to study their plastic, candy-filled eggs.

"You want to take the kids for half an hour while Summer and I do some shopping?" Kitty asked the men.

"Sure," Dad said quickly. "Want to go with me and your brother to meet the Easter Bunny, Rylee?"

"Okay," she said shyly, looking up at him.

Jake's chest tightened. This wasn't going the way it was supposed to. Instead of getting more distance between himself and the little family of guests, it looked like he and Dad and even his sister were both getting closer to Summer and the kids.

Not a good thing.

"Thanks so much for this," Summer said minutes later as she and Kitty strolled through River Haven's little downtown. It consisted of a two-block main street that ran alongside the park, with a grocery store at one end, and a couple of other streets that held shops and restaurants. Down one of them was the library and beyond that, the elementary school.

Kitty laughed. "I could see it in your eyes, when Easter baskets were mentioned," she said. "Believe me, I've done a few late-night runs when I forgot something for Mason."

She gestured toward the end of the block. "We'll hit Tiny's Hardware. It has a little of everything, and I know they have Easter stuff. If you need more, we can walk down to the grocery. Or are you a prewrapped basket type? No judgment if you are."

"No! I like to make their baskets myself. I'm kicking myself that I put most of my crafting supplies in storage. I would have personalized them and all, except…everything's been so crazy."

"I'm sure," Kitty said. "Not that I'd know. I've never moved farther than next door."

"You grew up here?"

"At the house where I live and at the guesthouse. It's a great place to grow up, a great place to raise kids."

"It seems to be." Summer glanced back toward the park. "We wouldn't have had such a nice holiday celebration back in our neighborhood in Pittsburgh."

"Speaking of Easter," Kitty said, "would you and the kids like to join us for Easter dinner tomorrow? We'd love to have you."

"Oh…" Summer had been planning on a PB&J picnic at a local state park. "I don't want to horn in on your family gathering."

"Honestly, we'd welcome it. Our holidays have been too quiet since Mom got sick. Mason, especially, gets bummed out when he hears other kids talking about their big family gatherings."

"I hear that." She hesitated. She didn't want to intrude, but Kitty seemed sincere, and she knew the kids would enjoy a bigger group for the holiday. "Thank you. We'd love to come. I'll help with cooking and cleanup. In fact, I could grab the stuff to make a bunny cake tonight, if you have cake pans."

"Dozens, in the guesthouse," Kitty said. "My mom made the prettiest cakes."

"You miss her."

Kitty nodded. "Every day. She was a free spirit, and so much fun." They stepped aside for a couple with two dachshunds to pass. "To be honest, Jake and I were closer to Dad. He was the steady one. But Mom was cut from a different cloth. One of a kind."

"I remember her from when we stayed here," Summer said. "She was beautiful."

"That she was."

They walked for a few minutes in silence, passing an antique store and a used bookshop. Summer resolved to come back and shop at both when she had more time and money.

They reached Tiny's Hardware, and as soon as they walked in, Summer realized Kitty had described it well. They had everything.

"Come meet Tiny first," Kitty said. "I see him in the back."

They walked to the back of the store, where an enormous man was lifting a window air conditioner with ease. Once he'd set it down on the floor, Kitty introduced him to Summer. "This is Tiny, who owns the place," she said.

Summer shook his hand, which was the size of a ham.

Kitty explained what they wanted, and Tiny directed them toward a display of Easter things. "Everything's on sale. We gotta make way for the next round of seasonal stuff."

As they browsed the Easter baskets, small plastic toys and stuffed bunnies, Summer seized the opportunity to learn more about the town. "Tell me about the schools here," she said. "Wyatt had a few struggles back in the city. I'm hoping it won't happen here."

"What kind of troubles, if you don't mind my asking?"

"Some teasing. Bullying."

"That's surprising." Kitty picked up a small metal truck and checked the price. "Wyatt seems like a kid other kids would like."

"He is," Summer said slowly. "But something happened, some family drama."

"Ah," Kitty said, nodding. "Sorry to hear it."

Just because she didn't pry, Summer wanted to tell her. If Kitty knew the situation, she might have some insight on whether Wyatt was likely to face similar problems here. Summer had heard more about the situation from Wyatt and from his teacher, and she was keen to avoid anything of the kind happening to him here. "This is for your ears only, but the kids' father turned out to have a whole other family, in another state. Word got out, and just recently, I found out that a couple of mean kids teased Wyatt, said he didn't have a dad, or his dad didn't want him, or was a criminal."

"How awful for you!" Kitty gave Summer a quick side hug. "I'm so sorry that happened to all of you. And my lips are sealed."

"Do you think it'll be a problem around here, if people hear what happened?"

Kitty looked thoughtful. "People are generally kind," she said, "but there are definitely a few who enjoy gossiping. River Haven is like everywhere else in that regard."

Summer nodded. "I appreciate the honesty. I'm going to do my best to get Wyatt started in school without anyone knowing our history."

"Good idea." Kitty stepped across the aisle and picked up a box of light bulbs. "Is your husband going to prison for this?"

Summer blew out a breath. "I don't know. I have an attorney, but honestly, he's a cut-rate one and I need to push him. Chuck is my kids' dad, though, and I'd hate to send him to jail."

"Not to mention it would affect his ability to pay child support," Kitty added.

"Right." And that was something she'd definitely needed her attorney to work on, because the amount Chuck had been paying her wasn't cutting it.

"By the way," Kitty added, coming back to Summer's side, "this job will throw you together with my brother a lot. I saw how he looked at you."

Heat rose to Summer's face. *How did he look at me?* she wanted to ask.

"Jake's vulnerable," Kitty went on. "He lost his wife, and she was pregnant, and it did a number on him. If he does make a move, just…be careful with his heart."

Compassion washed over Summer. "That must have been awful," she said. "Believe me, you have nothing to worry about. I'm not interested in anything but a professional relationship. Friendship at most. I picked a loser for a husband, and apparently a loser for a boss at my last job, since he turned out to be a creep. No men for me."

Did she sound too vehement? Maybe so. Maybe she was reminding herself as well, that Jake wasn't for her. No matter how nicely his muscles filled out the arms of his T-shirt. No matter how kind he'd been to her son.

As they took their purchases up to the counter, Tiny came over to ring them up. He crooked a massive finger to get them to lean in closer. "Just wanted you to know that Mrs. Stiffler was on the other side of the aisle while you were talking," he said.

"Oh, no." Kitty looked around. "Is she still here?"

"Rushed out," Tiny said. "Like she had news to share."

"Oh man. Thanks for letting us know." She turned to

Summer. "Mrs. Stiffler is one of the biggest gossips in town. If she overheard your story, it's just a matter of time until everyone else hears it too."

Summer's heart sank. She wanted to make a good life here, but if word of her past got out, would they face the same problems they were running from?

Summer mulled over the situation as they walked back to the park, stowing their purchases in Kitty's car, away from kids' prying eyes.

She wanted to make a great life for her kids. That was her entire goal. And she'd found this situation that seemed so good in many ways. Even now, she could see that Rylee was talking to Jake and his dad, sitting between them on a park bench. Wyatt was running around with Mason and another kid.

There were nice people here, and a decent home. It was the kind of place she could imagine staying for awhile. Chuck, her ex, was nowhere nearby, which was good.

But now, she'd let slip the story about her husband's bigamy. If word got around, would kids tease Wyatt again?

Her head spun as she tried to consider options. Maybe she'd jumped into the idea of staying on at the guesthouse too quickly.

The thought of returning to Pittsburgh made her stomach hurt. Finding a new job and a new home wouldn't be easy.

If they moved on to another location, they'd also have to start over.

Here, she had a job and a place to live. It had all fallen into her lap. But small towns were gossipy. There was no doubt in her mind that word of her family problems would filter through the town. And maybe people wouldn't care, but maybe they would.

Still, she couldn't keep running forever. And running from problems wasn't a behavior she wanted to model for her kids.

She needed to teach Wyatt how to handle teasing better. She knew it was all in the way a kid reacted, and she was pretty sure that Wyatt, in his upset state, had reacted badly, letting the bullies back in Pittsburgh know they were getting to him.

She had to make sure that didn't happen again. And it struck her: in Mr. Wright and Jake, she had a good resource of how men handled teasing.

She could ask them if they'd coach Wyatt a little on how to handle it. Because she wanted to stay here, she thought, looking at her kids' happy faces. She wanted, badly, to make this work.

Chapter Six

Roasting marshmallows wasn't the way Jake had expected to spend Easter night. But he couldn't complain. He himself had suggested it, and it seemed to be working.

Wyatt had looked more and more miserable as the day had gone on. Jake had asked Summer about it and learned it was due to Wyatt's nerves about starting school tomorrow.

That was normal. It wasn't easy to be the new kid in school. But there was more to it, according to Summer. Wyatt had experienced some bullying back in his previous school, and he dreaded the same thing happening again, here in the place where he hoped to start over.

In fact, Summer had asked for his help. "Wyatt needs to learn how to conquer his fears, to deal with them," she'd said. "My methods, like sharing my feelings with a friend, don't seem to work for a ten-year-old boy. Maybe you have a better way of coping, a man's way, to suggest."

He'd liked that she'd asked him. Liked it too much, in fact. But he did want to help.

So he'd suggested they have a campfire tonight. Doing something distracting was male method #1 for getting past fears.

Jake intended to focus on the goal of helping Wyatt, without getting emotional or romantic about Summer.

They were all sitting around the fire circle now: Jake and Summer, Wyatt, Rylee, Dad, Kitty and Mason. The fire circle, down in the yard halfway between the guesthouse and the river, hadn't been used much in the past couple of years, but ten minutes of work had fixed it up. They'd brought lawn chairs down, and Jake had gotten Wyatt to help him build the fire, using the old, dry wood stacked up under the deck.

Kitty's contribution had been marshmallows to roast, and it turned out that Rylee had never done it before. With some coaching from her mother, and one dropped marshmallow that had made her cry, she'd roasted a marshmallow of her own, let it cool and eaten it. The ecstatic expression on her face was reward enough for making this spontaneous event happen.

Soon Rylee was yawning in Summer's lap. "I'm taking Rylee up to bed," she said. "Wyatt, do you want to come in now, too?"

The boy shrugged. He was looking scared and miserable again.

"Stay out here," Jake suggested. "We'll hang for a little while and then I'll show you how to put out the fire safely. That's an important skill for anyone who's going to work with fire."

Wyatt perked up a little, and Summer gave him a grateful smile. Kitty and Mason headed for their house after a round of good-nights.

"Think I'll head inside, too, if you men have got this," Dad said to Wyatt and Jake.

"We've got it," Jake said, and Wyatt nodded.

When it was just the two of them, Jake raked through the fire, showing Wyatt how to spread out the coals so it would be easier to extinguish them. "Excited about your new school?" he asked Wyatt.

The boy didn't answer. He just poked at the fire.

"I never had to start at a new school," Jake admitted. "Lived here the whole time I was in school. I'd think it could be a little scary."

Wyatt gave a tiny nod, not looking at him.

"Everyone gets scared, doing something new," Jake said. "But that'll go away fast. The kids here are nice."

Wyatt still didn't speak.

This wasn't going well. "You'll have Mason," Jake said. "If not in your class, then at recess."

"Yeah," Wyatt said without enthusiasm.

"Watch the fire while I get another bucket of water," Jake said finally. He filled a bucket from the hose, brought it down. Wyatt was staring gloomily into the fire.

He showed the boy how to sprinkle water on the fire, and the hiss of steam got a smile and a "cool!" out of him. Then they were back to silence.

Jake felt awkward, but he wanted to help the kid.

"So, do you like the learning part of school better, or the playground?" he asked.

"Playground," Wyatt said quickly. "I'm not the best at reading."

"Like any sports in particular?"

"Baseball," Wyatt said in a voice so quiet Jake could barely hear him. "But I'm not that good at it."

No wonder the kid was nervous. "Have you had much chance to practice?"

"Not really," the boy said. "There weren't that many kids in our neighborhood, and I had to babysit Rylee a lot."

"There you go," Jake said. "That's why you're not good yet. You haven't practiced."

"You think if I practice, I could get good?" The hope in the little boy's eyes touched Jake's heart.

"I do," he said. "But it'll take time and dedication."

"What's ded…"

"Dedication. It's sticking with it and trying every day."

Wyatt nodded. "I can do that." He looked a little more optimistic.

"You know," Jake said, "I didn't do that well at school when I was your age. Math and reading were hard for me."

"Yeah?" Again, there was that hopeful, hungry look in the kid's eyes.

"Yeah. Everyone doesn't have to be good at everything. You just try your best, and pretty soon you'll find out what you *are* good at."

"Did you?"

"Uh-huh. Take that cup and put some more water on the fire," he said. "Just sprinkle it and hit the hot spots."

Again, the fire sizzled, and Wyatt smiled.

"Turned out I was good with cars," Jake said. "Made sense. My dad owned a car shop, and I followed in his footsteps."

"I like cars, too," Wyatt said. "I wish I could study that instead of books."

Jake remembered having the same thoughts himself, as a kid. He'd looked out the window of the classroom a lot, and when a cool car drove by, he'd been unable to look away. It had gotten him in trouble sometimes.

"You need math and reading to do a good job working on machines or motors or cars," he said. "You'll get better. I did. And you'll be glad to be good at reading once you're studying an automotive manual. Math comes in handy when you have to calculate gear ratios or tire sizes. You've got to be able to work with fractions to convert measurements."

"I guess," Wyatt said.

Jake still wanted to offer some practical, immediate advice. "Tomorrow, just walk in like you want to be there. Act happy. Fake it if you have to, and you'll do fine."

"Fake it like how?"

Jake prodded at the coals, making sure there were no live ones. "Pretend you love starting at a new school and that you know you're going to make good friends. Pretend you enjoy reading and math."

Wyatt made a face.

"Ah, none of that. Chin up and put on a smile." Jake demonstrated, then crossed his eyes, and Wyatt laughed.

Jake heard a twig break and saw Summer standing there. She was smiling. "Come on, Wyatt, time for bed," she said just as Wyatt gave a huge yawn.

The boy went without protest. Summer looked over her shoulder. "Thanks," she said quietly.

After they'd disappeared into the darkness, Jake cleaned up the fire pit, thinking.

He felt good, helping Summer. He'd often done the same for Mason, given his nephew a man's perspective on things. He liked providing that type of service.

And that was as much as could happen, he reminded himself. He wasn't going to have a son of his own to mentor. He had to content himself with helping other people's kids.

With a pang, he thought of the unborn baby his wife had been carrying when she'd died. He didn't even know for sure it was his child. But he still regretted the loss. If he and his wife had made it as a couple, he'd have raised the child, biologically his or not.

He sat down on one of the lawn chairs and watched the moonlight shine on the river. Listened to the gentle lapping of the water against the dock. Watched the rowboat bob, gently. Tried to empty away the negative and focus on what was good.

He had a lot of blessings in his life: work he loved, closeness with his dad and sister and nephew, a community that felt like home. He needed to value that.

"Hey." The smoky voice behind him brought every sense to attention. He stood and turned and there was Summer, her dark hair shining in the moonlight. She took a step toward him, then stopped. "I, uh, I just wanted to say thank you. For talking to Wyatt. He went to sleep quickly, and he didn't seem as worried. Whatever you said to him worked. And so did this." She waved a hand to indicate the fire circle.

"He's a good kid," Jake said. "He'll do okay."

"I hope so." She bit her lip.

He took a step toward her, and without thinking, he opened his arms. Would she step into them?

She hesitated, and then she did.

He folded his arms around her and kind of patted her back. *You're comforting her and that's all.*

But his heart disagreed. It was a very good thing that she quickly pulled back and went inside.

Summer was *not* going to think about last night.

She was in the kitchen, cleaning up from breakfast. In exchange for sharing the kitchen, she'd offered to fix some meals for Jake and his father, and so she'd made pancakes and bacon this morning.

She watched Mr. Wright clearing his plate. Next to him, Rylee was eating with enthusiasm, too, her third small pancake.

Wyatt had only eaten one, and then Mason had yelled that the school bus was coming, and Wyatt had run outside. Summer had wanted to go along, but an earlier call to the school secretary had confirmed that Wyatt's paperwork had arrived from their school back in Pittsburgh and that Wyatt would be in Mason's class. Summer had paperwork to sign, but she could come in and do it anytime in the next few days. It was a relaxed attitude that would never have flown back in the city, but Summer guessed she was glad of it. Wyatt had climbed on the school bus with Mason, like any other kid, rather than arriving embarrassingly with his mom.

Jake had scarfed down a big stack of pancakes and then he'd left too, with a quick, impersonal, "Be at the shop if you need me."

She actually did need to consult with him, make some decisions before moving forward with her new job. She wanted to cement her place here. To do great work and make herself indispensable. To do that, she needed to discuss her duties with Jake.

Mr. Wright had already told her that whatever she did was fine, but Summer didn't buy that. She was realizing that, for now at least, Jake was the decision-maker about the guesthouse.

Jake had been so great with Wyatt last night. His words of wisdom, and really just his reassuring presence, were the reason Wyatt had gone to sleep quickly and awakened in a reasonably good mood.

Jake had also been a big comfort to her. When he'd wrapped his arms around her, she'd felt like she had something to cling to, a life raft in the storm she was living through. His broad chest had felt so good to lean against, his arms so strong.

But she'd quickly pulled herself out of his embrace and skittered back to her suite. She knew from experience that men weren't to be relied on. She couldn't make that mistake again. Her kids depended on her to be strong and independent, not weak and needy.

So she was going to keep things professional. After Mr.

Wright had gone back to his suite, she set Rylee up with crayons and a coloring book and cleaned the kitchen thoroughly. Rain beat against the windows, and she felt inexplicably sad. Maybe she was just worried about Wyatt, or maybe it was the loneliness of having left behind her old life and now being in charge of creating a new one.

After cleaning the kitchen and having a brief exchange with the lawyer who was working on making her child support official, she couldn't wait any longer. She had to talk to Jake, get his input, before she could plan out her week's work. Since Mr. Wright had said he was going to take a nap, Jake was at bat.

She bundled Rylee into her rain gear, grabbed a few toys to keep her entertained and ran with her across the yard to the shop next door.

Inside, the customer area consisted of three old chairs beside a desk. The main building, where the work got done, was surprisingly large and airy. Jake was examining the hinges of a Mini Cooper that was dotted with rust. Another man, farther back in the shop, seemed to be stripping paint off an old car door.

"Hey," she said quietly, and then, "hey!"

"Mr. Jake!" Rylee yelled.

Jake jerked to attention. He put down his tools and came over. "You didn't need to come out in the rain," he said.

"I wanted to show you my rain boots," Rylee said, holding them out for his admiration. They were pink, with big white and green dots all over them.

He smiled down at her. "They're pretty," he said.

"Sit in the chair and look at your book," Summer ordered. Then she faced Jake. "I need to talk to you."

His eyes hooded. "I'm sorry about last night," he said.

"Don't be. That's not what I need to discuss." She brushed

past the concern in his eyes. "I need to lay out a plan for what to get done this week, and set a couple of time-based goals, too. I know you're busy, but here's what I'm thinking of to get started." She pulled out her phone and held it up. "I made a tentative list."

He moved close beside her and squinted at her phone. He smelled fresh, and at this angle she could see that his hair was still a little damp. There were a few threads of white in his beard and sideburns.

"Does that say attic?" he asked. But when she looked at him, he wasn't looking at the phone. He was looking at her. His eyes darkened.

She took a step away. "Maybe I'd better sum it up for you," she said, feeling breathless. "Um, I'm going to deep clean the front room and entryway today. I need to pull spring decorations out of the attic, too, and put away the Easter decorations."

"I can help with the attic stuff tonight," he said. "Don't try to bring it down by yourself. Clean some, but pace yourself. The guesthouse has been a mess for a good while. It doesn't have to be all fancy overnight."

"Okay," she said slowly. "I just like to keep busy."

"You're trying to keep your mind off Wyatt, aren't you?"

She wrinkled her nose. Busted. "I am. I wish I had a nanny cam to see how he's doing in the classroom."

"He'll be okay," Jake said, his voice gentle. "He has to go to school, it's mandatory. And you're not allowed to bring your mom with you." One side of his mouth quirked up, just a little.

"You're laughing at me." She fake-glared at him.

"No, not really. But you've sent him to school before, for several years. Is it worse than that?"

She thought back to that first day of kindergarten. How

she'd put him on the bus and then gotten in the car with her husband. They'd followed the bus to school, along with lots of other parents in the neighborhood. There had been pictures and tears, and she'd felt close to Chuck.

Had Chuck done the same with his other kids, in his other family?

She shook off the thought. "No, you're right, it'll probably be fine."

"It will." He reached as if to pat her arm and then pulled his hand back.

"Hey, Jake!" The shout from the guy way back in the shop got both of their attention. The man pointed.

Rylee was sneaking from the customer area into the shop.

"Rylee!" Summer rushed forward and grabbed her daughter, mentally berating herself. She'd taken her eyes off her child in a dangerous environment. That wasn't good. "You stay where Mom tells you to stay," she scolded.

Rylee started to cry.

The shop door opened, and a woman with a sour face and curly gray hair came in, walking quickly considering that she was using a cane. "I need to talk to you, Jacob Wright."

At least, that was what Summer thought she said. It was hard to hear over Rylee's crying. "Quiet down, honey," she ordered, shifting to support the weight of her.

"Hi, Mrs. Stiffler," Jake said. "How can I help you?"

The woman looked meaningfully at Summer and Rylee, and then back at Jake.

Rylee's wails got louder. She must sense Summer's tension.

Suddenly, she realized where she'd heard the name before. This must be the woman whom Tiny at the hardware store had said had eavesdropped on her and Kitty.

And Summer wasn't going to help matters by sticking

around with a screaming child. She shifted Rylee to her hip, wiped her hand on her jeans and held it out. "I'm Summer Jones," she said.

"I *know* who you are. Read all about it on the internet."

Summer didn't even want to look at Jake. "Well. I need to get this kiddo home." She grabbed Rylee's things and hurried out into the rain.

Was this even going to work? How was Wyatt going to manage if that awful woman was spreading the word about their difficulties already?

Chapter Seven

Jake stopped work at 3:00, way earlier than usual, and sent his mechanic home. He couldn't focus.

Having Summer and her kids living at the guesthouse had created all kinds of changes and posed all kinds of threats. And he wasn't thinking of the type Mrs. Stiffler was talking about.

What the woman had told him wasn't news. He'd heard most of the story from Summer already. He hoped he'd tamed the older woman's desire to spread the news by his nonreaction, but he wasn't counting on it.

Summer had seemed upset when she'd left with Rylee, and he wanted to make sure she was okay. Too, he was curious how Wyatt's first day at River Haven Elementary had gone.

Mostly, though, he wanted to protect his father from too much involvement with Summer and her kids. Summer didn't mean any harm, he was pretty sure of that, but Dad was vulnerable right now.

When he walked into the guesthouse, just as he'd feared, Summer and Mr. Wright were together. Summer was loading Easter decorations into a big box while Dad watched from his recliner.

Summer was flushed with her exertion, her dark hair carelessly tied back. She closed the box, shifted back on her heels and lifted it, swaying a little.

Jake rushed to help her. His father started to stand, too, but Jake waved him away. "I'll carry that upstairs," Jake said to both of them.

"I wouldn't mind a little help," she admitted. "But I want to start bringing down the springtime decorations from the attic. Maybe you or your dad could let me know which boxes to bring down first."

Rylee came into the living room then, rubbing her eyes. Summer started to put down her box, but Rylee climbed right into Dad's lap and stuck her thumb in her mouth.

Dad's smile was as broad as Jake had seen it in years. "I'll watch out for this pretty little lady while you all haul and carry," he said.

"You okay, Rylee?" Summer asked.

Rylee nodded and leaned against Dad's chest.

They carried the box up one set of stairs, and then paused so Jake could open the door that led to the attic.

Summer frowned. "I always think about how Wyatt needs male role models," she said, "but I think Rylee is hungry for male attention, too, as little as she is."

"Could be dangerous," Jake said.

They huffed up the next flight of stairs and set the box down against the wall.

"I know. She's been taught not to talk to strangers, but I'm a little concerned about how she's attaching herself to your dad."

"He's a good man, very safe," Jake reassured her.

Summer nodded. "I believe that. But he's *not* her grandfather, and who knows how long he'll be in her life? I don't want her—or Wyatt, either, for that matter—to suffer another loss."

That right there was a good reason for him and Dad to keep their distance. Jake had been thinking about it from Dad's end, worrying about his father being hurt emotionally. But it was also true that Summer's kids were vulnerable.

He looked around the attic, its hodgepodge of dusty suitcases and cardboard boxes and rubber storage bins stacked high.

"We need to find the tubs marked Spring, according to your dad," she said. "Seems like your mom was pretty well organized."

"In some ways." He scanned the boxes. The labels, in his mother's firm handwriting, tightened his throat.

"Here's one." She pulled out a tub and shoved it toward the door. "So what did that lovely woman have to say about me, out in your shop?"

He moved a couple of boxes to look at the stack behind them. "Same story you'd already told me. I didn't get excited about it like she'd hoped."

"So she's off to tell her tale to someone else," Summer said. "Wonder how long it'll be until Wyatt's new classmates start hearing gossip from their parents."

"People are mostly kind," he said. "If they do hear about it, most will think of you as the victim, like I do. You didn't do anything wrong."

"Unless stupidity is considered a crime."

Jake waved that idea away. "Most people know to take whatever Mrs. Stiffler says with a grain of salt."

"Don't listen to a word Mrs. Stiffler says." Dad stood at the entrance to the attic, breathing hard. Beside him, Rylee looked awed with the cluttered space. "She's a busybody. Always was in our business."

His father's comments surprised him. Dad rarely said a negative word about anyone.

"Your mother couldn't stand her," Dad went on. His face was red, whether from exertion or anger it was hard to say.

"Can I look?" Rylee took a step into the attic. She saw an old wooden rocking horse and ran toward it.

Summer intercepted her. "No, you don't, sweetie. We don't have permission to play with the old toys up here. They could be antiques."

"That rocking horse is pretty sturdy," Dad said, his face clearing. "We could clean it up and bring it down. Remember riding it, Jake?"

"*He* rode it?" Rylee stared up at Jake.

"When he was small," Dad said, smiling.

Jake added another box to the stack and looked around. He didn't see any other boxes marked Spring.

"This ought to do it for us, for now," he said.

They carried the boxes down, with Dad going ahead, holding Rylee's hand and promising he'd get the rocking horse cleaned up for her soon.

As they set the boxes down in the living room, the front door burst open and Wyatt came in. The school bus chugged away.

The boy threw down his backpack and went to the couch, where he pulled his legs up and grabbed the TV remote.

Summer sat beside him and gave him a quick hug. "How was day one?" she asked.

Wyatt's lip stuck out and he turned on the TV and turned up the volume.

"Uh-uh." Summer stood and took the remote from the child's hand. "You don't have to talk about what happened, but you can't be rude."

"Aw!" Wyatt looked ready to blow.

Rylee climbed up on the sofa and leaned against him. "It's okay," she said, patting his arm.

He pulled her into his lap as if she were a pet or a toy. He leaned his cheek against her dark hair.

"Did you find a friend?" Rylee asked him.

Summer handed the remote to Jake's father and started quietly unpacking a box. Obviously, she'd decided Wyatt's sister was better medicine than she was, and Jake tended to agree. Jake's father turned on a baseball game, keeping the volume low.

"I was bad at baseball and the kids laughed at me," Wyatt said.

Summer's face fell. It must be hard to hear your child sounding upset. Jake felt for the kid, too.

"Awww." Rylee patted her brother's arm again. "I sorry."

"Were there any nice kids?" Summer asked.

"Mason was nice," Wyatt admitted. "And some *girls*."

At Wyatt's age, the endorsement of girls was no good, Jake knew that. His heart filled with compassion. These kids had been through a lot and they'd obviously learned to comfort one another. "I can play some catch with you if you want," he said.

"I hate baseball." Wyatt wrapped his arms around his knees, pulling himself into the smallest possible ball.

"Remember," Jake said, "you can get better, but you have to practice."

Wyatt extricated himself from his sister and ran up the stairs, his feet pounding. A door slammed.

"Don't push him," Summer said.

"He needs to toughen up and try."

"Oh, and you know what he needs after, what, two days?"

"No. Sorry." He *did* know what boys were like, maybe better than she did, but she knew her son. He had no reason to get involved with her or the boy. Didn't want to, in fact. He wanted to keep his distance.

Summer looked upstairs, bit her lip. "Maybe you're right," she said. "Sorry to snap at you."

"Not a problem. You're worried about him."

"Always," she said with a self-deprecating smile.

They unpacked boxes together. Rylee squeezed into the recliner beside Dad, and he explained the baseball game to her. Most of it went over her head, but she didn't seem to mind.

"Any interest in some beef stew?" Summer asked after half an hour. "It's in the Crock-Pot and it's probably ready."

"You don't need to—" Jake started, although he'd caught a whiff that had made his stomach growl.

"That would be great," Dad said at the same time.

Wyatt clattered down the stairs. "I'll play catch," he said to Jake. "I'm sorry I was mean. Can we do it now?"

"After dinner," Summer said firmly. "We're having beef stew."

"Yay!" Wyatt flopped on the floor in front of the TV.

Yeah, great. So they'd have another meal together as a family. Afterward, he'd play catch with Wyatt. Rather than getting less involved with the little family, he and his father were both getting more so.

By Wednesday afternoon, Summer was so sick of playing dolls with Rylee, and so ashamed of plunking her in front of the TV way too often, that she questioned her own worthiness as a mother.

Of course, she adored her daughter and wanted the best for her. She was thrilled that Rylee seemed to be adjusting to their move.

But she hadn't realized how much she'd counted on other families in her old neighborhood: teenagers to babysit, preschoolers as playmates, and the way all the mothers helped one another out in a pinch.

The sense of community had gone a little wrong when word of Chuck's other family had gotten out. The close-knit neighborhood had turned into a hotbed of gossip, and some of her mom-friends had pulled away from her, seeming to think that the demise of her marriage might be contagious.

"Come *on,* Mommy, let's play!" Rylee tugged Summer by the hand, leading to the riverbank where Summer had agreed to have a picnic for Rylee's dolls. In addition to the couple of full-sized baby dolls Rylee had brought from home, she'd also been given a couple of Barbie knockoffs from the attic. Now, Summer spread an old blanket and watched Rylee arrange her four disparate-sized dolls in a circle.

It was a brisk, windy spring day. Scents from Kitty's daffodils and hyacinths wafted toward them. Kitty was at work, and the little neighborhood seemed to be deserted. The auto repair shop had seen a little activity earlier, but Jake had disappeared inside and the place was quiet.

He'd been kind enough to play catch with Wyatt for the past two evenings and had dealt with Wyatt's frustration, throwing balls directly into Wyatt's borrowed mitt and encouraging him when he caught a couple tosses in a row. He'd modeled throwing skills, showing Wyatt how to shift his weight and draw back his arm to get the most power behind each pitch.

It had been good of Jake to take the time. Summer had showered the man with appreciation and cookies.

Wyatt's new obsession with baseball meant he didn't play with Rylee as often, though, and Rylee missed him when he was at school. As a result, she was becoming fussy and demanding.

"Come on, Mommy, play," she ordered. "You be the babies, and I'll be the big girls. Now, sit down," she had one of her Barbie dolls say.

"Right now," the other Barbie added.

"Okay," Summer said, making the two baby dolls sit obediently.

"No, not there! And be quiet!" Rylee was always a bit of a tyrant when she played dolls. She especially loved the rare opportunity to lord it over her mother.

Jake emerged from the shop, and even from this distance she could see the big smile on his face. Was he as glad to see her as she was to see him?

But no, he wasn't looking at her. He was looking past her to another woman who'd pulled into the house on the other side of the inn, a house that had previously appeared vacant. Now, she was walking toward Jake holding a little girl of about Rylee's age by the hand. Jake held out his arms and embraced the woman.

An ugly wave of jealousy washed over Summer. The other woman was pretty, unconventionally so, with hair that was long on one side and buzzed on the other. She wore black slacks and platform sandals. A jewel-green shirt that set off her auburn hair. She was petite and curvy and gorgeous.

Summer looked down at her own clothes. Jeans that had fit her better when she'd had a few more pounds on her. A flannel shirt, worn thin, over a plain gray T-shirt. Practical canvas sneakers on her feet.

Jake and the woman talked for a few minutes, with Jake looking as animated as she'd seen him. Hmmm. So he *did* have a girlfriend, right here in the neighborhood. Well, good. Summer certainly wasn't interested in him for herself, no way.

Jake picked up the little girl, carrying her easily in one arm. The trio walked toward Summer and Rylee.

"Summer, this is Gemma Keyser and her daughter, Juniper," Jake said. "Gemma, Summer Jones and Rylee. They're staying at the guesthouse to help us get it ready to reopen."

"Nice to meet you," Summer said, determined to squelch that odd burst of jealousy. *She's pretty. I'm sure she's nice. She looks interesting.* Summer wasn't the kind of woman who got jealous of other women. She didn't feel herself to be in competition with them over men. That seemed ridiculous and old-fashioned.

Of course, as things had turned out, she *had* been in competition with another woman for Chuck's love. Moreover, the other woman had won.

A car pulled into the shop's gravel parking lot, and a horn tooted.

"Back to work for me," Jake said, and headed toward his shop with long strides.

Summer looked down at Rylee, who was leaning against her, staring at the other little girl, who was staring back.

Summer snapped out of her uncharitable mood and sank down to her knees in front of the other little girl. "Do you like to play dolls?" she asked, suddenly realizing this was a potential way out of Rylee's boredom. "Show Juniper your dolls, Rylee, and share."

"Oh my, that's Kitty's old Barbie!" The other woman sank down, too. "Look, Juniper!"

The two girls knelt on the blanket. "You can play," Rylee said, handing the other girl a big and a little doll.

Juniper took the two dolls and set them facing Rylee's two.

Summer got to her feet at the same time Gemma did, leaving the children to play together.

"So, you're living here," Gemma said.

"For the time being."

"What's your interest in Jake?"

Summer blinked. "He's kind of my boss, along with his

dad." Why should she defend herself to this woman? "What's *your* interest?"

"He's an old friend, and he's had a rough road," she said. "I'd hate to see him hurt."

Summer raised her hands, palms out. "He's at no risk from me," she said. "I'm through with men for at least the next decade. Have at him."

Gemma snorted. "Have *at* him? Honey, that would be like going out with my brother. Besides which, I'm just off a bad divorce."

Relief she didn't want to analyze filled Summer's heart and relaxed her shoulders. "I'm sorry you've had a hard time. Do you live here full time? We haven't seen you."

"We've been away visiting family. But I'm here for good now. I just got a job at the library."

"Oh, how cool. We love libraries."

"Us, too. The job is part-time, for now, but I hope to expand it to full-time pretty soon."

Rylee grabbed one of her dolls out of the other girl's hand and then looked up at Summer.

Summer gave her a stern stare. "Share," she ordered.

Rylee made a face and handed the doll back to the other little girl.

"Let's sit." Gemma gestured toward a wooden bench that faced the river, just up the bank where they could still see their daughters.

Summer followed her and sat down. "Any ideas about inexpensive, good childcare?" she asked.

"There's a preschool that operates out of the church, every morning. I just enrolled Juniper. Your daughter should join."

"That would be so great. I don't know if I have the funds right now, though. Is it expensive?"

"Nope. Church sponsored." She searched something on

her phone and held it out to Summer. "Here's the contact information. I can send it to you."

They exchanged phone numbers. "This will be a relief if it works out," Summer said.

"And if you ever need extra cash, I may be looking for a babysitter. Or even just to exchange childcare or have some playdates."

"That would be great," Summer said. "But…before you make an offer like that, you should know I'm already being gossiped about in the town."

"I do know. I heard." The woman shrugged. "No big deal, to me. I've attracted plenty of gossip myself."

That was refreshing. They sat for awhile longer, chatting about the town and watching their daughters run around, playing tag now.

Summer was happy to have more of a plan for Rylee. Even happier that she and this new neighbor might become friends. Moms needed friends as much as their kids did. No one could raise a family alone. She felt like she and Kitty were starting to become friends, but Kitty worked every day as a middle-school teacher.

A new neighbor friend, with a daughter Rylee's age, was just what she hadn't realized she'd needed. She shot up a quick prayer of thanks.

Chapter Eight

Summer woke up Saturday morning with a squirmy, churning feeling in her stomach.

She'd had a dream about Jake, a hazy, romantic dream of walking and laughing together. He'd been leaning down, maybe to kiss her, when she'd awakened with a jolt.

There was a reason she'd vowed to avoid entanglements with men. Two of them, in fact: her children.

She'd taken a risk and brought them here to Holiday Haven for a fresh start. Surprisingly enough, it was working. But if their hearts were broken and their lives upended again, she couldn't count on them healing so well a second time.

No. She had to make this situation work. And to do that, to make the good life they'd barely started to create grow into full bloom, she had to squelch any romantic feelings for Jake.

Rylee was now enrolled in preschool, and so far, she was loving it. Wyatt was obsessed with playing catch, sometimes with Mason and sometimes with Jake.

They were adjusting, and she desperately wanted to keep their lives going in a positive direction.

Sunlight slanted through the bedroom windows. Aside from the pleasant sound of birds singing, it was quiet.

Too quiet.

She sat bolt upright and looked over at Rylee's bed. Empty.

Jumping up, she pulled on a bathrobe and went out to the main room. No kids. Wyatt's bedroom was empty, too.

She rushed out of their suite and started down the stairs. Hearing the sound of Rylee's laughter, she stopped.

Wyatt laughed, too, and then she heard the deeper murmur of adult male voices.

The kids were okay. Whew. She went back into the suite, threw on Saturday clothes and brushed her teeth and her hair. Then she headed back downstairs.

Her kids were cuddled together on the floor in front of the couch, still in their pajamas. They each had a bowl of cereal, and they were watching cartoons. Mr. Wright was in his recliner, and Jake was at a desk in the back of the room, working on a laptop.

It was a blast from the past.

As a kid, Summer had rarely lived in one place long enough to make close friends. But there had been a couple of times when she'd been invited to sleep over at someone's house. Someone with an ordinary family. Getting up early to eat sugary cereal and watch TV had seemed exotic to her, and she'd loved it.

Jake looked up and spotted her. "Hope this is okay," he said. "The kids came down, and we thought you might like to sleep in for a change."

She actually couldn't remember the last time she'd slept in on a Saturday. Maybe that was why she felt so breathless and disoriented. "Thank you," she said.

"Once you have some coffee and breakfast, I have something I want to show Rylee," Mr. Wright said. "Wyatt too, if he's interested."

"Get coffee, Mommy, hurry!" Rylee reached up, and Summer picked her up and kissed her and blew a raspberry into her neck, making her giggle.

There was a knock on the door, then a boy's shout outside. "That's Mason!" Wyatt said. He jumped up and ran to the door. He spoke to someone, then rushed back. "Can I go out and play?"

"Did you finish breakfast?"

Mason grabbed his cereal bowl and tilted it, gulping the remaining milk and cereal. "Can I now?"

"It's his third bowl," Jake said, a smile in his voice.

Summer had to laugh. "Go on out," she said. "Wear a jacket."

Wyatt grabbed a hoodie from the coatrack and ran outside.

"I have a friend, too," Rylee said. "Her name's Juniper. Can I go play?"

"Not right now." Summer headed to the kitchen for coffee.

"We can see if she's awake," she heard Jake say, "but later. Gemma likes to sleep late."

An unwanted pang of jealousy twisted Summer's insides. How did Jake know that?

He's not yours to worry about. She poured herself a cup of coffee and looked out the kitchen window. Wyatt and Mason were already digging in the garden plot, presumably for worms.

It reminded Summer that she needed to do some weeding and prepare the soil for the flowers she wanted to plant. She had a vivid memory of the summer flower beds here, and she hoped to restore them to their former glory. Some rocking chairs on the porches would be nice, too. She'd talk to Jake and Mr. Wright about it.

Half an hour later, she, Jake and Rylee followed Mr. Wright to a small shed on the edge of the property. He didn't lead them inside, but instead knelt down, holding onto the short set of steps that led inside. He shone a flashlight under the shed.

"What is it, what is it?" Rylee jumped up onto the wooden steps, then off, then on again.

He held a finger to his lips. "Shh. Come here beside me and look."

Rylee rushed to his side and knelt down. Then she screamed. "Mommy! Mommy! Come see!"

"Quieter, now," Mr. Wright rumbled.

Summer knelt and peered under the shed. Small dark shapes moved around. Mr. Wright scanned his flashlight over the area.

"Kittens! It's kittens! See, Mommy?"

"I do see! Wow! How many?"

"I counted five," Mr. Wright said. He leaned back and held out a hand to Jake. "Help me up, son. These old bones can only take so much bending."

Jake helped his father up and then knelt beside Summer and Rylee.

"So she's at it again," he said. "How old, Dad?"

"Four or five weeks," he said. "They're playful and active. I've been putting food out for them and the mama."

"Can I hold one?" Rylee asked.

Jake looked up at his father. "Think we can hold them?"

"If she lets you." Mr. Wright reached into his pocket. "I brought out a can of sardines. Mama cat's always hungry." He opened the can and set it down.

"Pee-yew!" Rylee held her nose.

The mother cat lifted her head and then got to her feet and walked over, her underside swinging heavily. She started chomping down the sardines.

Jake lay down on his side, reached under the shed and pulled out a mewing black-and-white kitten. He swung upright and held it, his big hands gentle. The mother cat looked over and then kept eating.

Rylee sat on her knees in front of him and reached for the cat.

"Careful, honey. Let Mr. Jake hold the kitty, and you can pet her if you're gentle."

Rylee reached out and touched the cat, then petted it. Suddenly, an orange kitten came out and walked boldly onto Rylee's lap.

Rylee squealed. "Mommy! Look! Ow, she's hurting me!"

"Those little claws are no joke." Jake was laughing. "Here, put my jacket over your lap so the kitten can't dig in." He put down the black-and-white kitten and shrugged out of his jacket, then draped it over Rylee's lap.

"Good job being gentle," Summer said as Rylee petted the orange kitten in her lap.

"I love her," Rylee said. "I wanna name her Sherbet. Can we keep her?"

"They have to stay with their mama for now," Mr. Wright said.

"Can we keep her after she's bigger?"

Summer laughed. "We'll see," she said.

Rylee stood abruptly, spilling the cat off her lap. "Wyatt!" she called. "Mom says we can maybe have a cat!"

Wyatt ran over, followed by Mason. He exclaimed when he saw the kittens and got down on all fours to look at them. "Cool," he said, and then his face fell. "But we can't have one."

The mother cat had finished the can of sardines. Now, she came over and hissed at the kids, then batted the kittens back under the shed.

"She's telling us they've had enough," Mr. Wright said.

"Why can't we have one?" Rylee asked Wyatt.

"Dad's allergic, remember?"

"But Daddy's not here."

"Yeah," Wyatt said, "but when he comes back, he can't be around a cat."

Summer blinked as she processed what Wyatt had said. It brought an ache to her heart. "I don't think Daddy's going to visit us here," she said.

"No," Wyatt said, "I mean when he comes back to live with us." His eyes were clear and his tone was certain. "He won't like it if we have a cat."

Summer looked at her son and sucked in a deep breath. She'd thought he understood that Chuck had made his decision. But here he was, assuming his father would return. Wishful thinking, of course, but his certainty made her sad.

Clearly, adjusting to their new family situation was going to be a process. She put a hand on Wyatt's back and rubbed it, just briefly.

It wasn't the time, in front of Jake and his father and Mason, to have a serious talk about their new reality. But she'd need to do it soon, so Wyatt didn't go on building false dreams of the future.

She hated to take that confidence out of his eyes. Hated to knock him off the good path he'd started to walk. But it was her job as a mother.

Just like staying away from other men who could arouse their hopes was her job. Above all, she had to protect her children from any more heartache than they'd already experienced.

The evening after playing with the kittens, Jake came in from a grocery run and looked in at his dad, dozing in front of a baseball game in his recliner. "Summer asleep?"

"She took a walk," Dad said. "She was restless after her kids went to sleep. I told her I'd keep an ear out for any wakefulness. She left her suite door open." He looked up at Jake. "Said she needed to think."

Jake frowned, set down his bags. "She shouldn't be walking alone."

"It's River Haven," Dad said.

Jake kept his jacket on. "Uh-uh. I'll go out and catch up with her. For safety."

His father lifted an eyebrow. "Don't fool yourself."

He paused in the act of opening the door. "What do you mean?"

"You're following her because you want to. Because you like her. Which isn't necessarily a bad thing." He paused, then added, "Just be careful."

"I'm not getting involved with her," Jake said firmly. "Just making sure she's okay."

"Uh-huh." Dad waved a hand. "Go on, now."

So Jake walked in the direction he figured Summer must have gone, and sure enough, there she was up ahead. She walked slowly, hands in her back pockets, looking at the river.

He wasn't surprised she needed to think. He'd seen her expression when Wyatt had made that confident claim that his father would come back. It had upset her.

Was that because she knew her husband wouldn't come back? Or was Wyatt on to something?

A loon gave a woo-OOH call as it splash-landed on the river. The fragrance of spring, fertile and rich, rose up from the muddy ground.

Jake was getting closer to Summer, his strides longer and quicker than hers. Not wanting to scare her, he called out. "Hey, Summer."

She spun around, her hand to her chest. "Jake! What are you doing out here?"

"Dad told me you took a walk," he said. "I didn't like the idea of you walking alone."

"It's River Haven." She started forward again, slowly.

He fell into step beside her. "That's what Dad said. Guess I'm a worrier."

They walked together along the ledge of high ground above the river. The gentle sound of water over rocks was soothing. But Jake didn't feel relaxed. He felt on high alert and took deep breaths to calm himself.

He knew it was safe out here. That wasn't what his increased heart rate was about. No, it was about walking alongside this woman who'd intrigued him from the moment she'd showed up at the guesthouse.

On their left, a few lights shone from houses, and the occasional car drove by. A train clattered through, blowing its whistle. By the time it had passed, they were at the edge of town.

"Pretty night," he said.

"Uh-huh." She sounded preoccupied.

"Want to talk about it?"

She shook her head. "Not really."

"Okay." He continued alongside her, quiet now. He didn't want to interrupt her thoughts, but he wasn't going to let her walk out alone when it was nearing midnight.

"It threw me, Wyatt thinking his dad is coming back," she burst out. "I don't know why he thinks that. There's no way."

"He might." Jake kept his voice mild. "He has you and the kids. A pretty compelling reason to change his mind."

She snorted. "Not to him."

"You never know."

She looked away and walked faster. He kept up but stayed silent.

"I wouldn't take him back," she said finally. "I have to protect my kids."

"And yourself?"

"And myself."

They walked for a few minutes in silence. They were past town now. The trail was on a high bluff beside the river. On the other side, a stand of trees gave way to a field, stubbly with cut-off stalks of corn.

"How'd you get involved with him?" he asked, genuinely curious. Summer seemed like a pretty sharp lady, and he was curious how it had happened that she'd made such a poor choice of partner.

She glanced over at him. "I was stupid. And young."

"The two go together," he said. "At least they did for me. I could tell some major young-and-stupid stories on myself."

A quick smile crossed her face. "I'd like to hear them sometime."

"Yours first," he said.

She shrugged. "Okay. I was about to graduate high school, eighteen years old, and my parents went on a rafting trip down in West Virginia. The whole group was drinking. They got into some nasty rapids and…" She lifted her hands, palms up. "They didn't make it home."

Jake's heart lurched at the thought of an eighteen-year-old losing both parents. "I'm sorry. That must have been awful."

She nodded. "They were impulsive folks, not real responsible, but I loved them. My dad was amazing."

"What did you do, losing them both that young?"

"I was seeing an older man at the time. He helped me manage the details—funerals, bank accounts, rent and bills—and I was grateful for the help. He was in business, and good at all that stuff."

Jake blew out a breath. He could imagine what was coming. "And he took advantage."

She shrugged. "Not exactly. I mean, it wasn't like my parents had money. But I clung onto him, and he let me, and we got married. And pretty soon, I was pregnant with Wyatt."

"He shouldn't have let that happen."

"You're right, he shouldn't have. Because he was already married."

She'd told him that before, but hearing the details now, he was even more disgusted with the guy. "That's unbelievable."

"Right? Thing is, my upbringing was so unconventional, I didn't know what regular families were like. When Chuck traveled a lot for business, I figured that was what normal people with normal jobs did." She shrugged. "The marriage wasn't exactly a fairy tale, but it wasn't awful. I was able to just work part-time, and raise Wyatt, and then Rylee came along."

Jake was fuming. "And this whole time, he was seeing his other family?"

"Uh-huh. Like I said, I was stupid. It was actually the other wife that found out and came to see us. Last year, right before Christmas. She laid down an ultimatum—he could come home to her and her kids full-time, or he'd pay through the nose and never see them again. She felt cheated on, see, and I guess she was. She was his wife first. He caved in and left us."

Jake looked over at her moonlit face, trying to read it. Had she been devastated? Or had the marriage been weak enough that she was emotionally okay with it being over? "That must have been hard to deal with. As a wife and as a mom."

"Especially as a mom," she said. "Not like he was father of the year, but he was there some, and he loved the kids. And kids always love their parents, no matter their flaws."

"That's true." Jake had adored his mom, even though she'd made some serious mistakes. "Wyatt still hopes he'll come back?"

She nodded and shut her eyes, then opened them. "Apparently so. That almost killed me."

He put an arm around her. "You've been through a lot."

"Thanks for listening." She leaned into him, just a little. "It's good to talk it through with someone who's not going to judge. You aren't, are you?"

He slowed down and turned her to face him. He brushed back a strand of her hair. "No, I'm not going to judge you. You were just a kid, and grieving, when all this happened. He took advantage of your inexperience."

"I guess he did." She gave a humorless chuckle. "Did a number on my self-esteem, that's for sure."

Her eyes looked impossibly large. Her lower lip was fuller than her upper one. There was a sprinkling of freckles across her nose.

He couldn't take his eyes off her. "You're beautiful, you know. Beautiful and desirable. He was a jerk."

"Thanks," she said softly. "You don't have to say that, but it's good to hear."

He couldn't move away. "I want to kiss you."

She sucked in a breath. "Jake…"

"I know," he said quickly. "I won't, but just…know I want to."

Clouds passed restlessly over the moon, alternately bathing them in moonlight and shadow. Across the river, a deer walked to the water's edge and drank.

"Look," he said, pointing it out to her.

"Aww, beautiful." She looked up at him. "You said you wanted to kiss me. Why'd you say you wouldn't?"

"Because I'm not a good risk for a relationship," he made

himself say. "I fought with my wife. To the point where she got upset and drove recklessly and crashed."

She didn't look shocked. "Your sister told me about it," she said. "She also told me your wife was pregnant."

"Yeah." Relief that he didn't have to share that news himself warred with shame that Summer knew what he'd done.

"Was it really your fault?"

He nodded. "A man is supposed to protect his family."

"But you can't always do that. Your dad mentioned that you were overseas for awhile. Including when she wrecked?"

"Yeah, but—"

"And she drove drunk, right?"

He nodded.

"So she shares a lot of the blame. Unless..." She looked up at him, one eyebrow arched. "Unless you're a superhero who can control everything from the other side of the world."

That made him smile. He didn't buy her logic, but he was glad she wasn't too put off by what he'd done.

"And so," she continued, "you *might* be allowed to have a little fun and a little closeness in your life. Do you still want to kiss me?"

"I do," he said.

"Then...do it."

And so, he did.

Chapter Nine

Jake's kiss was like nothing Summer had ever experienced before. Not that she had experienced much kissing. Her husband had been her first and only. And probably it was because they had been married a while, but their kisses had evolved into quick pecks.

This was different.

Jake cupped her face so carefully. His lips on hers were gentle, exploratory. Something inside her woke up, reminding her that she was a woman—a young woman—a woman with feelings, deep ones.

He lifted his head and brushed a finger through her hair. "Is this okay?"

She loved that he had asked. "It's very okay," she said.

He wrapped her in his strong arms and kissed her again, a little more deeply. For a moment, the intensity of her own feelings nearly swept her away. But he seemed to feel her trembling and loosened his hold on her, whispering about how beautiful she was, how much he liked kissing her. It was heady. Intoxicating.

From somewhere inside, she felt a twinge of nerves. She'd been telling herself ever since the breakup of her so-called marriage that she wouldn't get involved with a man again, wouldn't risk it. This could be a mistake.

He stroked a hand down her back and kissed her cheek, her neck. She breathed in the clean woodsy scent of him and decided to ignore that silly, scared feeling inside.

"I think we better go back," he said finally, a smile in his voice. "We don't want to scandalize the town."

She felt breathless. "No," she said, laughing a little. "We shouldn't scandalize anyone."

They walked back. This time, he tucked her under his arm, and they walked together, in step.

"Tell me more about you," he said. "You said your upbringing was unconventional?"

That was a nice thing about Jake. He wanted to know her, cared what she thought and what her life had been like.

"Oh, I had a pretty unusual childhood," she said. "Actually, coming to the guesthouse was probably the most traditional thing we did."

"Really?" He sounded surprised.

She laughed. "We never lived in one place for long. A lot of the time, we actually traveled in a van kind of like the one I have now."

"Where did you live, mostly?"

"Wow, around here… We spent some time in West Virginia. There was a kind of commune there, a farm where a lot of people lived. We stayed there for a while, and it was a lot of fun. Lots of kids. But my parents really loved the West, so we spent the most time out there."

"Like where?" Jake asked.

"Rocky Mountain National Park was a favorite," she said. "That was fairly close to Boulder, where we also spent time."

They were walking slowly as they talked, and it was a novel sensation to her. When was the last time she had strolled and confided in someone?

"You must've loved it," he said. "I feel like a real small-town boy compared to you. I spent most of my childhood right here. Every now and then, a trip to the shore, but mostly we were here to run the guesthouse."

"I did love all the travel we did, in a way," Summer said. "I adored my father. He was happiest going somewhere new, and Mom and I were happy when he was happy."

"What was he like?" Jake asked.

"He was really something. So handsome, so charismatic. Everyone loved him. The room lit up when he walked in, and everyone loved to listen to his stories."

"That sounds a little like my mom," Jake said. "She was someone everyone was drawn to. She was so warm and funny and creative."

"Funny—we both had a parent like that," she said. "You're second fiddle, but you don't even care, right?"

"Yes, exactly."

They smiled at each other. Summer didn't think she'd ever met anyone who understood that kind of feeling until Jake. Their childhoods had been so different outwardly, but in some ways, they were alike.

They walked in a comfortable silence for a few minutes. Beside them, the river glistened with silver ripples as it flowed, lapping against the rocks along the shore.

He tucked her closer, kissing the top of her head. A warm feeling spread inside her. Cherished. She felt cherished.

"Tell me more about your childhood," he said.

"Well, let's see. We spent a lot of time in Sedona. There was this gathering called the Harmonic Convergence. I don't know—the Earth's magnetic lines come together there. All very woo-woo." She raised her hands and wiggled her fingers to illustrate. As an adult, she didn't believe in any of that, but a lot of people from her childhood had. "We also went to Bryce and Zion. Canyonlands. I kind of miss the country out there. It was so majestic, all the red rocks against the blue sky."

Jake was quiet. Then he said, "That's…odd."

"What?" She looked up at him. There was a slight tension in his shoulders that she hadn't felt before.

"Oh, nothing. Look, we're back."

And indeed, there was the guesthouse. It had seemed like no time to get there. Suddenly, Summer realized that she was cold. She shivered and wrapped her arms around herself, her hands clenching her upper arms.

"You're cold." He took her hand and tugged her inside.

It felt like coming back to daily life, and she wasn't ready. "I don't want to say good-night," she admitted.

"Nor do I." He turned her to face him. "But we have to."

He wrapped his arms around her and just held her for a moment. She laid her cheek against him, hearing his strong heart beating in his chest. She knew she had to take care of herself, but just for a moment, it felt like she had been able to give up that adult sense of responsibility and let him take care of her.

He touched her chin and kissed her again—so gently, so perfectly—that she floated all the way upstairs.

In church the next day, Jake couldn't keep his mind on the sermon.

The problem wasn't that Wyatt and Mason were fidgeting and making faces at each other, nor that his father kept dozing off.

The problem was Summer.

They were sitting in a row: Jake's dad, Jake, Wyatt and Summer, Rylee having gone to the little kids' Sunday School. In front of them were Kitty and Mason.

Summer wore a blue dress that fitted her well, the full

skirt sweeping past her knees. Her dark hair shone. She didn't look at him much, but he was ultra conscious of her.

He'd kissed her.

He'd held that beautiful woman and kissed her, and he couldn't get it out of his mind.

She'd felt so perfect in his arms, slim and strong. Her skin, when he'd touched her cheek, was so soft. She'd smelled like flowers.

Even better was that she'd seemed to like being held by him. The way she'd looked at him, the pink of her cheeks, the quickened breathing…all of it had told him she liked it. Liked him.

He wanted to hold her again, so much that he had trouble breathing.

Dad nudged him, and he realized he'd stayed sitting while everyone else was getting to their feet for the closing hymn. He stood and tried to focus on the words of the old hymn. *Love has come again, like wheat that springeth green.*

The refrain made him think of Summer.

Had love come again? He hadn't expected it, hadn't wanted it. But the way he felt right now…yeah. It was an awful lot like love.

He wasn't supposed to do that. Wasn't supposed to fall in love again. Now, he wondered if he'd ever been in love before. He could barely remember what he'd felt when he'd gotten together with his wife. Lust, for sure, but love?

The marriage had been a mistake, and maybe that was why he'd been a poor excuse for a husband. He hadn't been able to show his wife the love she needed, and because of that, she'd strayed. Maybe she hadn't really loved him either.

He'd believed her accusation that he was a terrible husband, but what if that was because of the incompatibility between them? What if it wasn't an inherent flaw?

What if he could give himself another chance?

He glanced over at Summer as the song ended and caught her watching him. She blushed and looked down at her hymnal. Just that little pink in her cheeks made his heart sing.

There was something that was nagging at him, though.

Those places she'd mentioned traveling with her parents sounded very familiar.

There was a stack of postcards his mom had shown him, right before she'd died. He hadn't looked at them closely because they'd brought uncomfortable, angry feelings he couldn't deal with while also helping his dad and sister cope with losing Mom. And of course, he'd had to cope with his own sorrow, too. What Mom had told him, when giving him the postcards, had disturbed him enough that he'd tried to push it out of his mind.

But he did remember some of the place names, because, against his will, they'd intrigued him. Sedona. Boulder. Bisbee, Arizona. Canyonlands. Bryce National Park.

Summer had mentioned some of those same places last night.

He shook off the coincidence as Pastor Kevin gave the blessing. The music swelled, and people started gathering their things to leave. Wyatt burst out of his seat and climbed over the pew in front of them. Mason laughed wildly.

"Wyatt!" Summer reached over and gripped her son's shoulder. "You know better than that. Behave."

"Sorry, Mom." The boy looked a little contrite. But as soon as she let go of his shoulder, he ran out of the pew after Mason.

Those places her parents had taken her, places they'd camped or lived, were gathering spots for folks seeking a countercultural lifestyle, or at least, they had been gathering spots twenty years ago. Surely it was just a coincidence that those were the same places in Mom's postcards.

Summer looked over at him, one corner of her mouth quirking up. "Sorry for my kiddo's behavior," she said. "Sitting through a service is hard when you're ten, but he knows better than to run and climb in church."

"Boys will be boys," Dad said. "I thought he and Mason did pretty well."

As they all sidled out of the pew, as Summer said something to Dad that made him laugh, Jake's heart burned inside him with longing for what probably couldn't be. He wanted to hold her again, but that wasn't all he wanted.

He wanted her and the kids to be a permanent part of his family.

He greeted friends and talked for a moment with Kitty. The church was emptying out fast. On a rainy April day, people didn't seem inclined to stick around.

"Jake, a word?" The pastor approached him.

Jake shook the man's hand. "Nice service," he said. He usually spoke to the pastor about the sermon, but he couldn't claim to have listened to it today.

"Glad you enjoyed it. Are you still able to work on the church bus next week? The seniors have a trip to Amish country scheduled, and I'd like to make sure it's in tip-top shape."

"I'll take a look at it tomorrow," Jake promised.

"Great, thanks. You doing okay?"

Jake studied the man. "I am. Why?"

"I noticed that things have changed over at the guesthouse. Glad to see your dad is coming to church again and that you've brought your new tenants."

"I'm glad about Dad, too," Jake said. Then, since the man seemed to expect more, he added, "Summer's going to be staying there awhile, helping us get the place operational again."

He glanced over. Summer was talking to Wyatt. Rylee had been in kids' church, deemed too wiggly to stay for the whole adult service. Now, she ran to Dad and started talking rapidly to him.

"Summer's pretty," the pastor said, and Jake looked at him sharply. The man was a little old to be admiring Summer, wasn't he?

"She is," he said, trying for an indifferent tone.

"How much do you know about her?"

"Are you…interested? She's just off a rough breakup."

"No, no!" The pastor's laugh was genuine. "I'm past all that. Just looking out for my congregation."

Jake filed away the "past all that" remark. He knew Pastor Kevin was a widower, but he was in his sixties, energetic and fit. Surely one of the church ladies would snag him sooner or later. "Summer used to come to the guesthouse with her parents, when she was a kid," he said.

"Ahhh. So that's why she seems to have made herself at home." The pastor raised a hand, indicating to someone that he was almost done. "Just looking out for your family, son. You've been through a lot."

As they gathered coats and umbrellas, Jake jogged out to bring the truck around. He didn't have many doubts about Summer, but he did have a few. The pastor's words had reminded him of his priority: looking out for his family.

How could he find out whether his weird ideas about his mom's postcards were valid?

Wyatt and Rylee bemoaned the rain as they drove the short distance back to the guesthouse. "I wish we could have the kittens," Rylee said mournfully.

"They're not big enough, sweetie," Summer said.

An idea came to Jake. "Do you have any photos of when your family used to come to the guesthouse?" he asked Summer.

"I do," she said. "I have a whole album, in fact. Want to look at it?"

"Mom showed it to us before we came, and we brought it along," Wyatt said.

Summer clapped her hands. "Let's get out old pictures. It'll be a good way to spend a rainy Sunday. Maybe you all have some old photos, too."

Jake smiled at her enthusiasm. She really was a delight. Just being near her made the sun come out, no matter the actual weather.

"Sounds like fun," he said. "After lunch, we'll pull out some photos and look at some really bad fashion choices we all used to make."

"Hey," Dad protested, "my leisure suits were a real hit, back in the day."

"Mom was a dorky kid," Wyatt said, laughing.

Jake pulled into the parking space in front of the guesthouse. Good. He'd alleviate his suspicions, and he'd get to spend the afternoon hanging out with Summer.

There was nothing he'd rather do.

Chapter Ten

Summer went out to the van to dig out her photograph albums. It was a good opportunity for her to cool off and think.

She was still floating over Jake's kiss. She hadn't been able to stop thinking about it. And he was thinking about it, too, she could tell. Now, he wanted to spend the afternoon looking at old family photos, which surely meant he wanted to take things further, didn't it? That wasn't the desire of someone who'd just shared a casual kiss and intended to move on. It was more like something a serious boyfriend would want to do.

And Summer wanted that deeper relationship, too. So badly. She longed to be back in Jake's strong arms. Longed to know him better, to cook meals for him and his dad, to go out on dates. To explore what could happen.

But. But.

She wasn't in the market for a man. She wasn't good at choosing them. Her husband had been a disaster.

And now, the stakes were much, much higher than when she'd been a lonely eighteen-year-old looking for someone to depend on. Now, she had two young hearts in her care. Wyatt and Rylee had been deeply wounded by what Chuck had done. She couldn't risk letting them get hurt again.

That was why she'd resolved to stay away from men and romance.

It had been an easier resolution to make when there'd been no one around who interested her.

Jake more than interested her; she admired him. He worked hard, was kind, cared for his family. A salt-of-the-earth guy who loved his small town and had deep roots here. And handsome? His brand of rugged good looks was exactly what she liked.

So what was she supposed to do? Follow the path she'd set, alone with her kids, or explore this new possibility Jake seemed to be holding out?

She pulled out the album and opened it. There were her mom and dad, risk-takers to the core. She didn't have that gene, didn't want to take risks that would give her kids an unstable life, possibly even leave them orphans too young, as her parents had done to her.

At the same time, her parents had been so full of color and life. She didn't want her own life, her kids' lives, to be completely monochrome.

She pulled the album against her chest and closed her jacket over it to protect it from the rain. Then she jogged from the van to the guesthouse.

Okay, Mom and Dad. I'll at least explore the rich, full, fun, colorful option. I'll give Jake a try.

After lunch, they all moved into the living room. Mr. Wright and Jake built a fire, since the day had gotten chilly, with a few snowflakes. "It's supposed to be getting warmer, not colder," Summer complained.

"That's why we don't plant our flowers and vegetables until Mother's Day around here," Mr. Wright said. "Always the risk of a cold day or a frost."

"I hope the flowering trees don't get killed," Summer said.

"Fruit trees should be okay," Jake said. "That big magnolia out on the side of the house will get nipped, though."

"Awwww, it's so pretty!"

"Happens almost every year," Mr. Wright said. "Nothing to do about it. That's the Laurel Highlands for you."

"Well, at least we're cozy inside," Summer said philosophically. She'd pulled out a puzzle for Rylee to work on, and Wyatt was being sweet, helping her put it together. Mr. Wright sat down in his recliner, glasses on his nose, looking through a couple of the Wright family albums he'd dug out of storage. He'd promised to try to find photos of Summer and her family.

Summer sat on the floor and leaned back against the couch, her album on her lap. Jake sat down beside her, close.

Point one in his favor, Summer thought. She liked that he wasn't afraid to be close. Although...she could imagine getting a little too warm, quickly. Already, she felt the color rising in her face.

He looked down at her just as she looked up at him, and they shared a secret smile. Wow, did he ever have a nice smile.

She opened the album and flipped through. Just the sight of her parents made a lump rise in her throat. What she wouldn't have given to have them know Wyatt and Rylee. Their absence was a permanent hole in the fabric of her life.

"You miss them, don't you?" Jake wasn't looking at the album; he was looking at her.

She swallowed hard. "I do," she said. "They've been gone over ten years, but I think about them all the time. Wish the kids could know them."

Behind the cover of the album, he squeezed her hand. "I'm sorry you had such a hard loss."

She nodded. Then, aware that Mr. Wright could look over and see them holding hands, she eased hers away and flipped backward in the album. "That's me, in front of the guest-house, in all my four-year-old glory," she said. "Do I look like Rylee?"

"Let me see!" Rylee rushed over and leaned in. Wyatt was right behind her.

"You do look like Rylee," Jake said.

She turned the album toward Mr. Wright, and he squinted at the photo. "Yes, it's true," he said. "Cute as a button, just like Rylee."

"A button's not cute," Rylee said.

"It sure is, honey." Mr. Wright was studying the guest-house. "I remember when we painted that porch," he said. "Looks kind of shabby here, but we fixed it up."

Summer didn't want to say it, but the porch was looking even shabbier now. She resolved to talk to Jake about painting it, or having it done.

"Show us when you were *my* age," Wyatt said. So Summer flipped forward in the album until she found a couple of pictures of herself at ten.

"We look a little alike," she said, showing him.

"Aw, I look more like Dad." Wyatt sounded glum.

Summer bit her lip. Wyatt did look like Chuck, but he obviously didn't want to be associated with his dad right now. She didn't know what to say.

Mr. Wright jumped in. "You know who else you look like?" he said to Wyatt. "Guy with your same name. Wyatt Earp."

"Who's that?" Wyatt asked.

Summer had heard of him, but beyond a vague Western association, she didn't know who he was.

"He was a great gunslinger and lawman in the Wild West," Mr. Wright said. "Look him up on your mom's phone."

So Wyatt did. "I don't have a mustache!" he said.

"Not yet," Mr. Wright said, a twinkle in his eye.

Wyatt flipped through the photos and read some of the captions. "*Gunfight at the O.K. Corral* is a movie about him," he said. "Can we watch it?"

"Maybe when you're older," Summer said. "It sounds a little rough."

Mr. Wright winced. "Shouldn't have gotten into that, maybe," he said. "I'm sorry."

"It's all good." She smiled up at the older man. She was just glad that Wyatt had gotten off the subject of his resemblance to his father.

Mr. Wright leaned over and looked at another photo in Summer's album. "There's a nice picture of Mom, Jake," he said. "Quite a looker when she was young. Well, she was always beautiful." He stared at the photo, his eyes watering up.

Summer squeezed his hand. "It's good and bad to look at the old photos, isn't it? You want to remember, but it kind of hurts, too."

"Exactly right, young lady," Mr. Wright said.

Summer flipped back to the beginning of the album, wanting to see where her parents' association with the guesthouse had started.

Jake pointed to a photo. "That's your dad?"

Summer looked. There he was, so young, so good-looking. "That's him," she said through a tight throat.

"I think I might remember him. I don't remember your mom, though." Jake was frowning as he looked more closely at the photo.

"Now that picture is from when your mother was pregnant with you, Summer," Mr. Wright said, leaning over to study the album from behind them. "Their first visit. She spent a lot of time resting on that trip."

"I remember she said she had a tough pregnancy," Summer said. "That's one reason she never had any more kids."

"She was a sweet lady," Mr. Wright said. "I remember she used to wear one of those mood rings instead of a wedding ring, and she was heartbroken when she lost it. We all helped her look for it, including you, Jake. You must've been eight or nine. We hunted and hunted, but we never found it."

"I remember that ring!" Summer smiled. "She wanted Dad to buy her another one just like it, but he surprised her with a real wedding ring instead."

She flipped through the pages, looking at her parents. "My dad was so handsome, and such a great guy," she said, "but look at his outfits. He was color-blind, and unless Mom picked out his clothes, he wore some wacky combinations."

"Mason's color-blind," Wyatt said.

"Yes, he is." Jake's voice was a little odd. Suddenly, he eased away from Summer and stood. "Well. I'd better get out to the shop."

They all looked at him. "Breaking up the party so soon, son?" Mr. Wright said.

"Yep. Have to." He turned and strode out the door into the rain, not even bothering with a jacket.

That was strange. Strange and a little bit disappointing.

"Guess he got tired of old photos," Mr. Wright said philosophically. "Me, I could look at them all day."

"I'm bored," Wyatt said. "Can I watch TV, Mom?"

"Um, sure, I guess so. But upstairs, so we can have peace and quiet down here."

"Me, too!" Rylee said. Both kids thundered up the stairs.

Summer put away the kids' puzzle. She took the old photo album and looked at a picture of Mom and Dad.

She'd been inspired to try and take a risk on Jake, inspired by the thought of her free-living parents. She'd thought it was going well for a moment there. And then he'd just up and left.

Had something upset him, or was he just an abrupt kind of person? She realized she didn't know him well enough to be sure. She'd keep an open mind, but his sudden departure today had put a slight damper on her enthusiasm for pushing ahead with the relationship.

Jake was soaked by the time he got into the shop, the drizzle having turned into a downpour while they'd been inside looking at scrapbooks. He turned on the heater and paced.

His mind reeled from what he'd discovered and what it meant.

Summer's father was the man who'd had an affair with Jake's mother. Jake recognized him from the awful image burned in his mind, when he'd walked in on Mom with a man who wasn't her husband.

Not only that, but the man was color-blind. Like Kitty's son.

Jake had done a little reading about color blindness when Mason had been diagnosed, mostly to learn how it affected sports performance and how to adjust for that. In the process, he'd learned that the condition was often genetic.

The logical conclusion was that Summer's color-blind father, not Dad, was Kitty's father, and that Kitty had passed the color-blind gene on to Mason.

And nobody knew it but Jake.

How could it have happened? How could Summer's family have continued coming back to the guesthouse in light of the affair?

She'd said her parents, especially her mother, adored the

place. Which surely meant that her mother didn't know about the affair. Obviously, Summer didn't either.

Later, apparently, Summer's father had sent postcards to let Mom know his location. Was that out of emotional attachment? Wanting Mom to write him or visit him? Concern for the child he'd fathered?

He paced the shop restlessly, picking up tools and putting them down, unable to focus on anything. Not with big questions hammering at his mind.

The primary one being: How could he get involved with Summer now, knowing this secret that involved both their families?

He could keep the truth locked in his heart. That would mean listening to Summer talk about her wonderful father without showing his disgust at what the man had done. It would mean hiding something big from a woman who already had trust issues with men. If she found out the truth and knew he'd kept it from her, it would hurt her. And if she was hurt, her children would suffer, too.

On the other hand, he could tell everyone involved the truth. Tell Summer her father had cheated on her mother. Tell Kitty that the father she'd grown up with, the father she'd adored, wasn't really her father. Tell Dad that his wife hadn't been true to him.

Neither option was tenable.

Oh, Mom, why did you do it? His parents had had a good relationship, from what he'd been able to see. They'd worked together, laughed together, raised kids together. When Mom had gotten sick, Dad had refused outside nursing care until the very end, insisting on taking care of Mom himself.

How had Mom gone through life looking at Kitty, knowing that she wasn't Dad's child, but the child of a man who'd been passing through? Had she known Summer's dad was color-blind and had passed that genetic trait on to Kitty's baby?

He couldn't imagine keeping this enormous secret while being involved with Summer. But giving up the sweetness he'd glimpsed when he'd kissed her…that was a sacrifice he could barely force himself to make. He *wanted* to be involved with her. Wanted to be her man.

He kept coming back to the big barrier: if he didn't tell her what he knew, he'd essentially be lying to her. If they got involved, and then later, she learned the truth, she'd be crushed. Not only because she idolized her father, but because Jake had hid something huge from her.

He pounded the wall with his fist. Then he walked over to a cluttered corner of the shop and started moving parts around, organizing, straightening things up, getting it all into order.

It was heavy work, and by the time he was finished, he was sweating and breathing hard. And he had his answer.

He didn't like it—hated it in fact—but he was going to have to end things with Summer before they'd even begun. He was going to have to retract the loving feelings he'd shown her and tell her it wasn't going to work.

It would hurt her, sure. She liked him, was attracted to him. He knew enough about women to understand that.

But she'd get over it. Beyond a brief disappointment, his pulling back wouldn't cause any long-term damage. He already knew, from his wife, that he was a bad risk as a partner. Somehow, he'd lost track of that in the heady sensation of kissing Summer. But now, it was an ugly sort of consolation: she'd be better off without him, anyway.

If he pulled away from Summer, then he could keep Mom's secret to himself. He could avoid hurting Kitty and

Dad. He could allow Summer's impression of her father to remain intact.

It was the right thing to do. But the very thought of it carved a hole in his heart. He sat down wearily on a stack of tires, let his head sink into his hands and gave in to despair.

On Tuesday morning, Summer dropped Rylee off at preschool and then walked slowly back toward the guesthouse, stewing.

Sunday night, yesterday and this morning, she'd managed to act cheerful for the kids. Now that they were both in school, though, her annoyance with Jake took over her thoughts.

He'd ignored her since Sunday. She'd even worked on the porch outside the kitchen yesterday, scraping paint, knowing he'd have to come that way to go from the guesthouse to the shop. But he'd strode past with a glance and a quick wave.

What was wrong? Wasn't he even going to tell her? Could a guy ghost someone he was living with?

Summer was sick and tired of men treating her like she was completely unimportant.

Down the road, she spotted Jake walking in her direction, cutting through the town park, head down. She'd heard him telling his dad he was working on the church bus this morning. Mr. Wright had said he'd cover the shop this morning, not actually working on the cars, but watching over things and talking to customers.

It was the first time she'd seen Mr. Wright take an interest in the shop. He'd started the business, and she remembered from childhood visits that he'd worked hard there. One day, when she and Kitty had been playing together, he'd come out of the shop with greasy hands that he'd jokingly held out toward them, fake-threatening that he'd get them dirty. He'd delighted in their screams and giggles back then.

Since she'd arrived almost three weeks ago, Mr. Wright had stayed in the guesthouse, ignoring the business. Today's offer suggested he was coming out of his depression. That made her happy, and it had to make Jake even happier.

Except Jake didn't look happy. He looked slumped and gloomy and miserable. Why was *he* miserable?

On an impulse, she cut across the park and intercepted him. "Hey," she said, blocking his path.

He stopped, met her eyes and looked away.

"What's going on?" she asked.

"What do you mean?"

Was he serious? Did he think his behavior was normal? "Why'd you go cold on me?"

He straightened and seemed to gather himself. Finally, he looked her in the eye. "I shouldn't have kissed you. It was a mistake. We can't be together."

She'd expected something of the sort, and yet the words hit her like a blow. She swallowed hard. "Can I ask why?"

He sighed. "It's complicated."

Her husband, explaining the fact that he wasn't actually her husband, had used the same exact phrase. Heat rose in her face and she propped her hands on her hips. "You're seriously going to leave it at that?"

He winced and looked around the busy park. "Are you sure you want to do this here?"

Maybe she'd spoken a little loudly. Maybe she'd even yelled, because a couple of ladies in workout clothes had slowed down their power walk and were staring. The cook from The Hungry Hubcap was outside, leaning against the building's wall, watching them.

A public fight would be embarrassing. People would talk.

But Summer had one advantage over Jake: she'd been the subject of gossip for the past six months. She was hardened to it. "You've been avoiding me. Where else was I supposed to talk things through, in your shop while you're sawing apart a car or something?"

His mouth quirked up just a little at the corner, and then the hint of amusement was gone. "You're right. I'm sorry about avoiding you."

She waited. A robin hopped along the grass beside them. In the little pavilion, a toddler cried, and his mother pulled him into her lap. The mother was watching Jake and Summer, too.

Jake didn't volunteer any more information. He just stood there, shoulders slumped, head slightly bowed, still holding his toolbox. That thing had to weigh a ton, but apparently, he didn't want to commit to this conversation enough to put it down.

"Didn't you like kissing me?" she asked in a low voice. "Didn't you feel something?"

Three older gentlemen watched them from a pair of park benches, drinking coffee.

She glared at them, then at Jake. "Why'd you do it if you were going to act like *this* afterward?"

He was looking at her steadily now, his expression sad. "I liked it too much, Summer. You're a wonderful person—"

"Oh, no, you don't," she interrupted him. "Spare me the *you're a wonderful person* argument."

"I don't know what to say. Except that it's not going to work."

She crossed her arms over her chest and looked away. The bunny rabbit nibbling bright green grass, the squirrel chattering from a tree branch, the row of fragrant hyacinths, all of it suggested springtime happiness that was totally at odds with how she was feeling.

Have some pride, she scolded herself. *If you have to beg, you don't want him*. "Are you firing me, too?" she asked.

"No!" He looked startled. "No, Summer, we have a commitment. I hope you'll stay and help with the guesthouse."

"Don't you think that'll be a little awkward, living together? Won't you feel uncomfortable when you bring your girlfriends around?"

He shook his head slowly. "Believe me, that won't be happening."

"How about when I bring my dates home?" she taunted. She had no intention of doing that. She was never dating again. She just wanted to hurt him.

His eyes darkened and his fist clenched.

She took a step back, suddenly aware of how big he was, of his broad shoulders and muscular arms and powerful, working man's hands.

He relaxed his fist, shook his head like a dog shaking off water. "I need to get to my job."

So this was it, then. Their discussion was over, and it had let her know that there was nothing between them, couldn't be. Tears pushed at the backs of her eyes.

"Are you okay?" he asked quietly.

"I'm fine." She looked away so he wouldn't see the tears that were threatening to spill over. "Just go."

He stood for a moment more. She didn't look at him.

Finally, he turned and headed toward the church.

Feeling foolish and abandoned, Summer turned in the direction of the guesthouse. She didn't look around. Didn't want to see the curious, or even sympathetic, expressions of the surprisingly large number of people who were enjoying the park this morning. She took a step. Stumbled. Caught herself.

Gemma, her neighbor, took her arm. "Hey, Summer. Come on. You look like you could use a cup of coffee."

"I have to work," Summer said, resisting Gemma's tug. She wasn't going to abandon her plan to finish scraping the guesthouse's main porch just because her heart was breaking. *She* kept her commitments.

"Then we'll get together later. We'll take a hike. I'll pick up the girls from preschool and get a sitter for them."

"But…" Summer trailed off.

"I won't take no for an answer."

A hike with pretty, happy Gemma was the last thing Summer wanted, but she didn't have the emotional energy to refuse.

"I'll see you at one o'clock. I'll come get you."

Summer nodded. "Okay," she said through a tight throat. "One o'clock. Thanks." At least someone wanted to be her friend.

She'd thought Jake was her friend, but apparently, she'd been wrong.

Chapter Eleven

At the church, Jake went over to the rusty school bus that served as group transportation. He walked around it, studying the paint job and the headlights and brake lights.

His stomach churned. He hadn't thought talking to Summer would be easy; he'd known it would be a difficult conversation. That was why he'd been avoiding it, which was cowardly. He deserved what had happened: having it out with her in front of the whole town.

He'd hurt her and he hated it. The expression on her face, when she'd realized he wasn't going to explain and he wasn't going to change his mind, had nearly broken him. She'd stopped looking angry and started looking both miserable and resigned. She'd given up on him.

Which was the right thing for her to do, but it had just about killed him.

When she'd confronted him, all angry and indignant, he'd longed to pull her into his arms. To tell her it had been a mistake, that he did indeed want to kiss her again, that he felt not just something, but a whole lot, for her. All of which was absolutely true.

And yet he couldn't open that door again, and he couldn't explain why. It had been incredibly hard to ignore her for the past couple of days. Each time he'd seen her, it was as if there was an invisible magnet pulling him toward her. Resisting that pull had taken all his strength.

He felt exhausted and downhearted. Angry at his mother and Summer's father, for putting them into this untenable position, where being together would hurt a lot of people.

He wanted to be with Summer. She apparently wanted to be with him, though at this point, she'd most likely changed her mind.

What else could he do, though, to avoid hurting Dad and Kitty and Summer herself? He had to continue on the course he'd set out on. That was all there was to it.

Kneeling down, he looked under the bus, and the sight of its axles and springs and shock absorbers calmed him a little. This was what he had. This was what was real. This was how he was going to distract himself from the massive ache that had lodged in his chest.

"Hey, Jake, thanks for coming out." It was Pastor Kevin, spry and silver-haired, wearing his weekday uniform of jeans and a bright-colored polo shirt. Today's was purple.

Jake stood and shook the man's hand. "Glad to do it. Was just going to take a look at those brakes. You said you have a creeper?"

"Donated." The pastor motioned toward the church, where the rolling platform was beside the entrance.

Jake started toward it, but the pastor touched his arm. "Sit a minute first," he said. He opened the bus door and gestured toward the steps. He himself sat easily on the ground.

Jake felt creakier than the older man appeared to be. Probably just the misery. He sank down onto the bus steps.

"Need to talk about anything?" the older man asked.

Jake's bad mood must have shown on his face. "No," he said. The last thing he wanted to do was talk to the pastor, about Summer or anything else. He wanted to forget about her and focus on mechanical things he could understand and fix. "Thanks, though," he said belatedly, realizing he'd been abrupt.

Pastor Kevin was undeterred. "Heard you had a confrontation in the park this morning."

Jake's jaw dropped. "You already heard about that?"

"I hear about a lot of things," he said. "More than you'd expect. In fact, I may know as much about your family as you do. Maybe more."

The pastor had something on his mind. Apparently, Jake wasn't going to get to work in peace. "Yeah?"

"Yeah. So what was the argument about?"

Jake looked at the little church he'd attended his entire life. He'd been baptized there, and married there, and he expected to be buried in the little cemetery behind it.

The church was white with green shutters and a steeple that made it the tallest building in River Haven. Not that that was saying much. It was surrounded by mature trees. Bushes with red flowers dotted the base of the building.

Kevin had been the pastor there as long as Jake remembered. He'd probably planted those bushes. Jake knew for a fact that he'd built the stone wall that surrounded the church on two sides.

"You don't have to tell me if you don't want to," the pastor said. "I'm not in the business of forcing confessions."

Jake sighed. They said confession was good for the soul, and his soul could use some work right now. "I made a stupid mistake," he said.

"Related to our new friend Summer Jones?"

"Yeah." He looked down at his hands. "I couldn't resist making a move, getting closer. Which I shouldn't have done. It's not going to work out."

"Why not?" The pastor's expression was interested, but not nosy. More like compassionate.

"Family history."

They sat for a moment in silence. The pastor didn't seem surprised by Jake's words. He picked up a stick and started scraping at the ground, absently. Then he looked up at Jake. "Did you know I talked to your mother a fair amount when she was sick?"

Surprised, Jake met the other man's eyes. "No, I didn't."

"Uh-huh. She told me some things that had happened, things she'd done that she wasn't necessarily proud of."

"Yeah?" Jake really, really didn't want to talk about the things his mom had done.

Pastor Kevin twisted the stick he was holding. "She also told me that if you ever came to me, I should feel free to share what she told me. She thought you might need to talk. Same for your dad and Kitty."

Jake grabbed a wrench from his toolbox and tossed it, flipping it end to end. "Did Dad talk to you?"

"No. Not yet, and maybe he won't." He shifted into a cross-legged position. Man was limber. "She said something happened when you were about eleven."

Jake blew out a breath. "I don't remember much about that."

"Just as well," the pastor said promptly. "She hoped you didn't understand what you'd seen."

Jake's face went hot with remembered embarrassment. He'd heard a noise in one of the empty guest rooms and walked in, thinking they had an intruder or that the cat had gotten shut in the room.

Instead, he'd seen his mother with the man he now knew was Summer's father. Locked in an embrace. Clothing askew.

They'd jumped apart, and Jake had taken off, confused

and disturbed. His mother wasn't supposed to be kissing anyone but Dad.

Later, his mother had asked him if he had any questions. Mortified, he'd said he didn't, and she'd told him it would be best if he forgot about what he'd seen, that it wasn't important.

Being a young boy with fishing and baseball and cars on his mind, he mostly had.

A couple of months afterward, she'd announced she was going to have a baby. She and Dad had both seemed happy, and Jake hadn't thought much about it. Years later, when he understood more about life and pregnancies and babies, he'd had a fleeting, curious thought: what if Kitty wasn't actually Dad's daughter?

But the idea had made him squirm and he'd pushed it aside.

The pastor was looking at him expectantly. "Did she ever tell you the whole story?"

"Some of it." Another memory he didn't want to revisit. "Right before she lost consciousness for the last time, she told me that Dad wasn't Kitty's father. She gave me a stack of postcards from the man who actually was. There were no names, just addresses on them. Contact information in case she needed him, I guess."

"Did she tell Kitty at the same time?"

"No. We both thought she was too fragile, going through her divorce. And too attached to Dad, or the man she thinks is her father. Losing Mom and the biological connection with Dad… Mom thought it would be too much, and I agreed."

"And Summer's father is the man you saw with your mom," the pastor said. "He's Kitty's father."

Jake stared at him, stunned at the leap he'd made. "How do you know that?"

The minister looked out over the church parking lot and then returned his gaze to Jake. "When you've been in this business as long as I have, you get pretty good at putting two and two together," he said. "Your mom told me a few things about the man she got involved with. And when I was talking to Summer after church last week, she told me about her history with the guesthouse."

"Does everyone in town know?" Nothing would surprise Jake at this point.

"No, definitely not," Pastor Kevin said. "Why don't we take a look at the bus?"

Relieved to be done with this uncomfortable discussion, Jake got the creeper and slid under the bus. He examined the brakes, looked a couple of other things over and then slid back out. "You need new pads and rotors," he said. "I could fix up the worst of that rust, too."

"If you have time. Keep track of your hours. I'll pay you."

Jake shook his head. "You can pay for parts, but the labor is my contribution."

"You're a good man." The older man offered a compassionate smile. "All of that business with your mom shouldn't be on your shoulders. I'm sorry it is. How did you figure it out?"

Jake told him about the family photo albums, and how Summer had mentioned her father being colorblind, just like Wyatt. "Summer idolizes her dad. Thinks he was a great man." He paused. "Kind of like my dad thinks Mom was a great woman."

The pastor sighed. "People are people. We're all sinners."

"Right." Jake rubbed at a spot of rust on the bus. Then he turned to the pastor. "Telling the truth would devastate Dad and Summer both, and Kitty as well. It can't come out. Please don't tell anyone."

"I wouldn't."

Relief washed over Jake. One disaster averted, anyway.

"What are you going to do?" the pastor asked. "Do you plan to tell them, eventually?"

Jake shook his head. "That would be cruel."

"Secrets are toxic," Pastor Kevin said. "That's what I told your mother, and that's what I'm telling you."

"But when the truth would cause all kinds of pain..." Jake sighed. "What do you do when there's nothing right to do?"

The older man patted his shoulder. "I don't know the answer to that, son. I wish I did. But there's someone who does know that right path." He pointed at the sky. "Will you let me pray for you?"

Jake was feeling plenty disgruntled with God right now, but he didn't want to be rude. "Can't hurt anything," he said, knowing it was an ungracious response. What could prayer do to fix the mess he was in?

But as the pastor's strong voice rang out in prayer, asking God to show Jake the right path, asking Him to heal the hurts caused by his mother's actions and her secrets, Jake felt a little bit of peace seep into him.

Even so, he couldn't justify revealing the truth when it would hurt so many people. If he kept the information about his mother and Summer's father to himself, yes, *he* would hurt, because he couldn't have the thing he wanted: a relationship with Summer. But he was strong enough to bear it.

So bear it he would.

Summer answered the knock on the guesthouse's back door at 1:00. True to her word, Gemma stood there in hiking clothes.

"I don't know if I can—"

"I brought both girls back to my house and fed them

lunch," Gemma interrupted, talking fast. "They let me, since I was listed on your pick-up sheet. My little sister came over to babysit. She's twenty and loves kids, and they're having a blast. Want to check on Rylee before we head out?"

Clearly, Gemma wasn't going to let Summer out of this excursion. So Summer agreed to go, provided Rylee was okay about hanging out at Gemma's house.

She slid her feet into sneakers and followed Gemma to her place, where Gemma's daughter and Rylee were playing dress-up with Gemma's sister. Rylee was having too much fun to do anything more than wave distractedly, so Summer decided it was okay to head for the trailhead with Gemma. An hour or two in nature might, just might, help her feel better.

She'd cried a little as she'd scraped old paint from the guesthouse porch, and she still felt awful about the scene with Jake this morning. Awful because she'd *made* a scene, but even more awful because of what Jake had said. *It's not going to work.*

The idea that this little spark between them was never going to be anything more made her heart ache. But the fact that her livelihood and her kids' happiness depended on them staying right where they were at the guesthouse—basically living with Jake—was what worried her.

Maybe if she unburdened herself with Gemma, she could get herself together and figure out what to do.

After they'd walked for a few minutes, Gemma spoke up. "So, what was your big fight about this morning? I'm not being nosy. Well, maybe a little." She flashed Summer a quick smile. "But you need to know that everyone at preschool pickup was talking about it. You at least need to come up with a good story, before people start making things up."

Great. The other moms were talking about her. Was that

going to affect the kids? "I'm an idiot. I should never have confronted Jake there, but it was the only place I could make him talk to me. He's been avoiding me at the guesthouse."

"I could see you were upset afterward," Gemma said. "Are you still?"

"Very," Summer admitted.

They turned onto a path that ran alongside the river, with a wooden sign denoting it the Riverbend Walk. It was an extension of the path she and Jake had taken from the guesthouse, and just thinking about that walk, and the kiss that had come in the middle of it, made Summer's stomach churn.

She lifted her face to the cool breeze and listened to the soothing rush of the river. "Cone of silence?" she asked. Summer didn't even know if she could trust Gemma, but she had to talk to someone, or she was going to lose it.

"You can trust me," Gemma said. "Believe me, I know what it is to be the target of gossip and innuendo."

Summer glanced over at Gemma. "You do?"

"Uh-huh, but that's a story for another day," Gemma said. "Right now, it's your turn to talk."

Summer took a deep breath and let it out. "Okay," she said. "The other night, Jake and I, well, we kissed."

Gemma squealed, then clapped her hand over her mouth. "Sorry, it's just that Jake hasn't shown interest in anyone since his wife died."

"I shouldn't have done it. My husband…" She trailed off, not sure if she wanted to go there with Gemma.

"Go on," Gemma said. "I need the whole story."

The sun was warm on Summer's back now. Up ahead was a wooded section, with branches arching over the trail and the beginnings of green leaves visible in the undergrowth. A couple of squirrels chased each other across the path.

"So my husband turned out to not really be my husband,"

she said. "When we got married, I didn't realize that he had a whole other family, including a legal wife, in another state."

"Oh, you poor thing," Gemma said. "And the kids! Those poor kids."

"Yeah, especially since he abandoned all of us when he got caught. I mean, he says he wants to see the kids, but so far, it hasn't happened. It may be just talk on his part. Even if he tries to set up something specific, I'm not sure whether to let him see them. I mean, what if he starts talking about his other kids that he's living with now? How will that make them feel?"

Gemma shook her head. "Wow. That must be so hard to deal with."

Summer took off her jacket and tied it around her waist. "Yeah, so I'm a little shell-shocked. I should never have gotten close to Jake, but I really liked him, and we were really attracted to each other."

"I got that impression when I saw you together at church," Gemma said.

Great, it was obvious to other people. "Anyway. Getting to our argument today. After we kissed—which was pretty great, I'll admit that—Jake started avoiding me. This morning, he told me it couldn't go anywhere. He wouldn't say why. He just said, and I quote, 'It's complicated.'"

Gemma groaned. "Noooooo. Not that awful line."

"Right? What's worse is that my so-called husband used the same line."

"Get *out.* Girl, now I'm impressed you didn't punch him one."

Summer laughed. "Believe me, I wanted to." She made a fist and punched it into her other palm. "*Bam.* Couldn't he at least be original?"

"Typical guy." Gemma's forehead wrinkled. "I'm sorry to

hear that he was a jerk. When I saw how he looked at you… well. I thought you guys would make a good couple."

Summer's heart gave a little leap. She really, really wanted to ask Gemma to tell her more about that. Wanted the evidence that Jake did feel something for her.

But the way Jake had looked at her was not important. Not if everything was too *complicated* for him to have a relationship.

They walked along in silence for a few minutes. The steady rhythm of her feet, the green trees and bright sunshine, and most of all, the presence of a friend beside her made Summer feel marginally better.

"So are you going to do anything? Make any changes?"

Gemma's question snapped Summer back into her worries. "I don't know what to do," she said. "If Jake and I are at odds, how can we keep living at the guesthouse? For all I know, he'll fire me. I mean, he said he wouldn't, but I'm not sure I believe him."

"If he said he wouldn't, he won't. Jake is a trustworthy guy."

"Maybe. I hope that's true, because another move right now would be really rough on the kids."

"Yeah, they do seem to be settling in well. And Mr. Wright loves having you here."

The thought of the older man, the way he listened to Rylee and encouraged Jake, gave Summer's heart another tug. "He's great. He's the grandfather my children never had."

"I really hope you stay," Gemma said. "It's great having you guys next door."

"Thank you. You're a good neighbor, too." As they turned around, Summer impulsively gave Gemma a side hug. "Thank you so much for bringing me out. It helps to talk about it."

"Of course! We all need someone to talk to."

They picked up the pace, the only sounds the nature around them and their own breathing. Summer tried not to think, to just focus on moving her body and experiencing the warmth of the sun.

As their houses came into view, though, she spoke up. "I'm just so disappointed that Jake is falling into the same category as my husband. I didn't think he was a bad man, but I guess I was wrong."

"He's not a bad man," Gemma said. "I've known him forever, and I can't believe that."

"Well, he's being a bad man to me."

"I can see why you feel that way." Gemma nodded. "Oh, honey, I'm sorry. He wouldn't do this without a reason."

Summer didn't comment on that. He must have a reason, true, but that didn't keep it from hurting.

"I'll be praying for you and the kids," Gemma said.

"Thank you. Thanks for this." She waved a hand. "It's so beautiful here."

Her throat tightened on the last word. She did love it here. She loved the natural beauty of the place. She loved the small town, the guesthouse, the opportunities for her kids. "I really want to stay," she admitted.

"Then stay and see what happens," Gemma said. "Help them get the guesthouse into shape, at least."

"I'll think about it," she said. "And thank you so much. You've been a big help."

Summer did think about it for the rest of the day as she sanded the porch, cooked dinner with Rylee's help and watched Wyatt play baseball. And tried not to look for Jake.

Talking to Gemma had helped, but she still felt off balance. Every time she thought about Jake and his words, her stomach twisted and her whole chest ached.

Which was a huge overreaction to a guy she hadn't even known very long. No doubt she was bringing in her feelings about what her husband had done.

That didn't stop her from hurting. Jake was special, and what she'd felt for him was different than what she'd felt for anyone before. It had seemed like the real thing.

It wasn't. Which meant that living here, with this man she yearned for but couldn't have, was going to hurt every single day.

What to do?

She had her kids to think about, which meant she needed to take stock, to look for options.

The trouble was, there were no good options. If she moved out of the guesthouse, quit the job and went somewhere else, where would she go? What would she do for work? And how would the kids react to another move? It just wouldn't be good for them.

On the other hand, staying here just might break her heart.

But even as she thought that, she knew she'd made a decision. Yes, her heart might be a little broken, but that was better than having her kids' lives torn apart again. She had to think of them first, and what was good for them right at this moment was to stay where they were—in this safe environment, making new friends and having some stability and fun.

Maybe she and Jake would end up being able to be friends, and it wouldn't hurt anymore. Maybe this situation could last at least until the guesthouse got going and her finances stabilized, at which point she and the kids could find another place to live, close enough not to upend their lives again.

So that was it, then. They'd stay in the guesthouse. And she would try to have a cordial, non-emotional relationship with Jake.

Chapter Twelve

Jake walked into the kitchen on Friday afternoon for his meeting with Summer. It had been more than a week—nine days, if anyone was counting—since his big blowup with her. She'd said this would be a good time, when her new child-care exchange with Gemma gave her the ability to focus.

He'd worried that he and Summer wouldn't be able to work together. He'd worried that she and the kids would leave, taking with them the plans for the guesthouse and, more importantly, Dad's newfound cure from depression. He couldn't have blamed her for leaving, or at least acting nasty, after he'd been so cold in the park that day.

But to his surprise, Summer had been professional, and even, as the days went by, pleasant. He'd tried to live up to that and mostly managed. Maybe the pastor's prayers helped. Maybe it was his own, because he'd been praying plenty.

The kids helped, too. He and Summer couldn't stay too distant or cool with them there. Dad was a good buffer, too. As a result, his interactions with Summer were getting back to some kind of normal.

Today would be the test. They were going to meet one-on-one to finalize plans for the Open House, happening in just over two weeks on Mother's Day. The event would re-introduce the guesthouse to the community, paving the way for their grand reopening. Today, in addition to pinning down the plan and figuring out what his role would be, Jake's goal was to work professionally with Summer, keeping things friendly but distant.

Sun slanted into the kitchen, casting squares of light onto the wooden table. Before Summer had come here to live and work, the table had been cluttered and dusty. Now it was polished to a rich shine, with a glass jar full of tulips as a centerpiece.

There were blue-and-white curtains at the windows. Rylee's artwork and Wyatt's latest math test decorated the front of the refrigerator. It was like a whole different room, warm and full of life.

Summer came in through the door, wearing jeans and a rose-colored shirt. "Got Rylee settled at Gemma's for an hour," she said. "Just let me grab my stuff and we can get started." She hurried over to the small desk she'd set up in a corner of the kitchen and grabbed a tablet and pen from it.

She was pink-cheeked, her hair a little messy. She was beautiful.

Jake drew in a breath. *Friendly and distant.* "I was just noticing how nice the kitchen looks," he told her. "It feels like home. Like how my mom had it, awhile back."

She smiled. "Thanks! That's great to hear. Speaking of moms…" She frowned down at her tablet.

Jake's heart nearly stopped. What had she found out about his mom?

"Tell me a little about how this Mother's Day Open House used to work," she said. "We're not doing the same thing exactly, since this is to reintroduce the guesthouse to the community. But it would be nice to follow some of your mom's traditions."

Relief made his shoulders relax. He thought back, remembering how his mother had prepared for the holiday. "The main thing was, Mom set up places for kids to play outside, lots of games, and she put food and drinks out there. She made the dads go out and take care of the kids, play with them. She said what most moms needed was a break."

"Amen to that," Summer said. "Go on. What would she do for the moms, once the kids were taken care of?"

"Tea and scones," he said. "She'd traveled some, before she met my dad, and she wanted to make it sort of British. Made a big deal of getting fresh cream and whipping it herself. Different kinds of jams, and she did little sandwiches too. The moms loved it." His throat tightened. His mom had been at her creative best, planning events like these, bringing something special to their small town.

"Sort of sweeping them away on a little vacation," Summer said. "It's a terrific idea. We could do our open house the same way. Except..." She trailed off, then spoke again. "Since it's happening on Mother's Day, what should we do about people who aren't moms but want to be? Or who lost a child, or lost their mom? I'd like to include everyone in this, to show that the guesthouse is a welcoming place."

"I'm not sure how she handled that," he said. "I think it was just for moms. But we can change that, if you want."

"Hmmm." She looked thoughtful, tapping her pencil on the table. Then she looked up and met his eyes. "How do you feel about Mother's Day, since you lost your mom recently?"

He hadn't thought about it, but this would be his first Mother's Day without his mom. Last year, she'd been so sick. He and Kitty had brought in a bunch of flowers, and written cards, and sat with her. Dad had broken down and had to leave.

He looked away and took a couple of deep breaths, making sure he wasn't going to embarrass himself and cry or something.

"I'm sorry." Summer reached across the table and touched his hand, gave it a quick squeeze. "If this is going to be too hard—"

"No, no, it's good." He shook his head rapidly. "Man, I didn't know it would hit me like that. But I want to do it. Carry on her tradition." He frowned. "Maybe have a place where people can get away from the crowd if they're emotional."

"With candles and quiet music." She looked thoughtful. "Maybe that back parlor nobody ever uses, that looks out on the field? And we could have a tribute wall where people could write memories."

He winced. "That sounds kind of depressing."

She lifted her hands, palms up. "I mean…it's a depressing day for some people. But we don't have to say it's just for grieving. We could call it the relaxation room, or something. If Mother's Day is a quiet day for them, there's a place for them here."

He nodded slowly. "You know what," he said, "I think Rylee's kittens will be ready to come inside by then…"

Her eyes lit up. "Yes! Like therapy animals. Nobody can be too sad with kittens around. Although…will they be able to sit still and be comforting? They seem pretty active."

"If they're too wild, we'll take them out. Maybe find a teenager to be in charge of them."

She clapped her hands. "Perfect. This way, we can open it up to the whole community. Encourage everyone to come, not just those who want to celebrate Mother's Day."

Their gazes tangled, and then he found himself looking at her pretty mouth. Her pretty, kissable mouth. He should know, because kissing it, and holding her in his arms, had been the best thing he'd done in years.

She raised her eyebrows and he looked away to hide the way she tugged at his heart. He knew it couldn't go anywhere, but he just plain liked being around her.

"What do you need me to do?" he asked.

"You're putting me in charge?"

"Absolutely." He pushed her pad of paper back toward her.

"Okay," she said. She picked up the pen and started jotting down notes. "You organize the dads and kids. Not that all moms who come will bring a dad along. I'm sure some single moms will come. But there should be enough men to take charge of the kids. You can make Wyatt your marshal. And Rylee loves to be in charge, so give her a job, too."

"On it." He liked the idea of being in charge of the dads and kids. It made him feel a part of the family-oriented community in River Haven.

She smiled at him. "So this means it's really happening, right? I can start taking reservations for the summer?"

"Yes. But how will anyone know we're reopening, until the open house?"

"I was thinking of sending mailers and emails to all the past guests whose contact information we have on file. Let them know that Holiday Haven is accepting new reservations again."

"That's a great idea." What would they have done without Summer managing the reopening?

Shouts came from the yard, and then the back door burst open. It was Wyatt. "Mom, guess what! I made the River Haven Reds! Just like Mason!"

Summer jumped up and hugged him. "That's wonderful! You worked so hard and it paid off!"

Pride pushed Jake to his feet. The kid *had* worked hard

on his throwing and hitting skills. Not only had he practiced often with Jake, but he'd also recruited Mason to throw a ball around with him. When no one had been available, he'd thrown a tennis ball against the wall of the shed, over and over. Kid had persistence. "Good job, buddy," he said, and gave Wyatt a high five.

As Wyatt described the details of the tryout, all kinds of feelings washed over Jake. Almost a fatherly pride, but also an ache, because he wouldn't be a father, and couldn't be one to Wyatt.

Summer hugged Wyatt again. "Thank you, for helping him," she mouthed over his shoulder.

Jake nodded, feeling his smile stretch wide. To see her joy, and Wyatt's, to know he had a hand in putting those smiles on their faces…yeah. He was a goner. He cared way too much about this little family.

As she sat in a lawn chair a week later, watching Wyatt warming up with his teammates, Summer realized she'd never felt happier.

Only part of the reason was that Jake was beside her.

It was a warm Saturday night at the town ball field, located on the edge of River Haven. Even though this was just a community league, lots of local people showed up for the first practice game.

Rylee had stayed home with Mr. Wright. They'd both begged, saying they wanted to look through Mr. Wright's postcard collection and make popcorn and bring the kittens in for a trial run. They'd promised they'd come to another game.

A couple of men came over to Jake, and he stood to speak with them, greeting them easily, laughing at something one of them said.

Summer watched him thoughtfully. He was comfortable in his own skin. Comfortable talking with anyone, from wealthy customers at his shop, to the pastor, to this pair of dads who were still wearing work shirts from a local heavy equipment company. He was great with Wyatt, and Rylee, and his own father.

He wasn't a wealthy banker or doctor. Didn't wear a suit. Didn't talk about himself much.

But his worth and character shone out from him. He was respected by everyone in town. In fact, for a week after their public argument in the park, Summer had felt a distinct chill from some of the townspeople who'd previously been pleasant. Only after she and Jake had been seen interacting on a friendly basis, in the hardware store and at the Italian restaurant with the kids and Mr. Wright, had people warmed back up to her.

Summer wanted to make a great life for her kids. That had been her intention when she'd come to the Holiday Haven Guesthouse five weeks ago: to give them a fun spring break trip, and to figure out how to extend that into a long-term, good life.

God had smiled on that goal. Here they were, a part of a strong community. She had a job and a place to live. Wyatt was laughing with his teammates, including Mason, who'd become a good friend. As Wyatt waited for his turn at bat, he seemed worlds different from the sullen kid he'd been when they'd arrived. Rylee was doing well too; tonight, she was back at the guesthouse with the kind man she'd claimed as a stand-in grandpa.

None of it would have been possible without Jake.

A family group came and set up lawn chairs beside Summer. She smiled at them, and then Wyatt's team got a hit, and she and Jake and the new family stood and cheered.

Then three kids in a row struck out, including Wyatt. The parents around her groused that the other team's pitcher was too good, that he looked too old to play in this league.

Jake shouted encouragement along with her and the rest of the parents, and threw out an "it's okay" when Wyatt struck out. He was invested in Wyatt, because he'd helped him learn to throw and catch. Something Wyatt's own father hadn't taken the time to do. And to be fair, she hadn't, either. Jake had done something kind and useful for her son, just because he was a good guy.

She'd thought she had to stay single and independent for her kids' sake. But what if that wasn't so? Wyatt wouldn't be here tonight without having Jake in his life.

A woman from the other group offered Summer a drink from their cooler. Jake had moved off to one side to talk with an older couple whom Summer had seen in church.

"I'm Jasmine," the woman said. "This is my sister Tara, and this is our mom, Mary."

"Tallest kid out there is mine," Tara said, "but no one would mistake him for being older. He's skinny as a rail."

"First base," Mary, the grandmother, added, and then they all watched as the tall, lanky kid tagged a player out. Cheers rose, loud from the family who'd just introduced themselves, desultory from the rest of the crowd. People were getting into socializing, paying less attention to the game.

"So are you and Jake, like, a *thing*?" Tara asked.

Summer hesitated for a little too long before shaking her head.

"It's okay, it's not my business." Tara waved both hands to indicate that Summer didn't need to say more. "It's just, he's a nice guy. And he was so heartbroken when his wife died."

The other two women nodded.

"Personally," Tara said, "I didn't see why he was so sad."

"Tara!" Jasmine said, but without much energy. She leaned forward in her lawn chair to look at Summer. "See, Jake was away, serving our country, and his wife was running around with like three different men. Openly!"

"They weren't well suited," Tara said. "He was a straight arrow, quiet, and she was, how should I say it, fun-loving."

"Just like his mother," Mary said. "Like a lot of men, he married someone like his mother."

"He's better off without his wife," Jasmine said. When Summer blinked at the harshness of the statement, she shrugged. "What can I say. She was a bad wife."

"Which doesn't mean you don't grieve," Mary said. "There may have been unresolved issues between them."

A cheer broke out and Summer jumped up with the rest of them, standing on tiptoe to try to figure out what had happened.

"Yeah, Wyatt!" a couple of people yelled, Jake included. He came back over to stand beside her.

Wyatt and his team were running in from the outfield.

"What did Wyatt do?" she asked Jake as they both settled into their lawn chairs.

"Socializing rather than watching the game?" He looked amused. "Your son just caught a fly to end the inning."

"Yay, Wyatt!" she called belatedly.

Jake laughed at her. Their chairs were close together now, and so she saw when his laughter changed to something else.

He looked into her eyes, and then his gaze dropped to her lips. Just for a second, but *wow.*

She blinked and turned back to look at the game. And then Jake leaned close to her. "We're going to have to do something about this," he growled in her ear, sending a delicious chill down her spine.

* * *

Back at the guesthouse, cleaning up the mess Rylee and Mr. Wright had made, she thought about what Jake had said. *When* were they going to *do something* about that spark between them? Tonight?

Both kids were in bed. After a perfunctory offer to help clean up the postcards, books and dress-up clothes he and Rylee had gotten out, Mr. Wright had headed for bed, too.

If Jake tried to kiss her again, would she let him?

It had led to his withdrawing before. But he sure didn't seem to be withdrawn now.

She moved faster around the room, smiling, picking up dress-up clothes and folding them. She shouldn't be optimistic, but that was her nature. She was impulsive, known for it. Sometimes made bad mistakes because of it.

A smarter woman would have waited, would have discussed everything in detail with Jake before going forward at all.

But she'd been so disappointed in men for so long, and here was Jake blowing all those bad impressions out of the water. And being so handsome and kind.

She scooped up a pile of postcards set apart from the others Rylee and Mr. Wright had been looking at. Where would he want these stored? She straightened them into a neat stack and set them on the table beside his recliner.

The edge of one postcard caught her attention. That strange, loopy T looked just the way her father had used to write it. Weird. Unable to quell her curiosity, she pulled out the card and studied it.

It *was* her father's writing.

Thinking of you all. Address is 16 Juniper Way, Taos, Arizona, 87529.

Huh. She hadn't thought Dad was a good correspondent,

nor close enough to Jake's parents to send them a card. She looked at the rest of the cards in the stack.

Each one started with an innocuous greeting, and then gave an address. Boulder. Spokane. Sedona.

Even Pittsburgh.

What in the world?

Holding the stack, she went into the kitchen where Jake was making himself a cup of coffee. "Hey, I just found something weird," she said. "Do you know anything about these postcards from my dad?"

Chapter Thirteen

Jake turned around slowly. The warm kitchen around him, the aroma from the cup of coffee he'd just brewed, the dishes he'd been about to wash…all of it faded away.

All he could see was Summer's confused face and the postcards she held in her hand.

Oh, no.

His stomach knotted painfully. How had she gotten ahold of those?

Why hadn't he put those postcards way, way back in some box in the attic? Why hadn't he thrown them away, burned them?

Instead, he'd tossed them into a box with Dad's postcard collection.

He was an idiot.

"This is my father's writing." She walked closer and held out the postcards. "And it's our addresses." She flipped through them. "See? We lived in Sedona, and in Boulder, and in Spokane…" She looked up at him. "Any idea why my dad was sending these?"

His mind raced. Should he tell her the truth? When it was going to shock and hurt her?

Maybe he should make up some big story about why her

father had stayed in touch. Maybe he could be convincing enough that she'd believe him.

But keeping quiet about the truth was one thing. Making up a lie was another. That was definitely wrong, and he wasn't willing to do it.

So his goal had to be damage control. The least pain for everyone involved.

He sucked in a deep breath, went over to the table and pulled out a chair. "Sit down," he said. "I have a story to tell you, and it's going to be hard to hear."

For the first time, concern came into her eyes. She frowned, staring at him, and then sat down at the table.

He sat catty-corner from her. A train chugged by on the tracks across the road, its whistle a mournful sound.

Don't be a coward. Out with it.

"During that first visit your parents had here, when your mom was pregnant with you, something happened."

"Okay…" She waited.

How to frame it so her father wasn't portrayed in a totally negative light?

"Jake. Go *on*."

There was really no way to pretty it up. "Your dad, and my mom…they, um, had an affair."

Her mouth dropped open.

"I really don't know what led up to it. What else was going on in their lives."

She shook her head slowly, back and forth, back and forth. "How can that be true? What would make you think that?"

Jake felt like the kid who hadn't studied before an incredibly important test. Why hadn't he prepared for this eventuality, figured out what to say and how to say it?

She made a rolling motion with her hand, the universal "go on" signal.

He swallowed hard. "I, uh, I was eleven at the time, and I actually… I walked in on them."

She gasped. "You walked in on them in bed?"

"Not exactly." He hesitated. Thinking of your parents being intimate was practically impossible for most people. But a worse thought was one of your parents being intimate with someone outside the marriage. "How much detail do you want to know?"

She lifted her hands, palms up. "All of it, of course! I just don't believe this." She shook her head in that stunned way again. "I just don't believe it," she said, more slowly. "You must have misunderstood what you saw."

"They were partly undressed. Kissing."

She cringed, her neck sinking down into her shoulders. "I mean, my dad was a wild man, and I know he and Mom fought sometimes. But I never thought… I heard a few accusations, but…" She looked up at him, her cheeks going pink. "Are you sure they really, um, consummated the affair?"

He blew out a breath. Nodded. "I didn't really understand what I'd seen, at the time. But later, when she was dying, she told me. She wanted someone to know, because—" He broke off.

"Because why?" She met his eyes, her own gaze steady. It was as if she'd steeled herself for the worst. As if she already knew what that *worst* was.

She was strong, and she deserved the truth in a direct way. "Because she got pregnant. With Kitty."

She continued to stare at him. In the background, the hum of the refrigerator sounded loud.

There was no pink in her cheeks now. She'd gone pale. Too pale.

"Let me get you something to drink. This has been too much for you." He got up, poured a glass of cold water from the pitcher in the fridge and handed it to her. Grabbed his own coffee cup and sat down again.

She sipped water, then put the glass down and stared at it, unseeingly.

Jake would have given anything to spare her from this bombshell. She was clearly trying to process it, but the implications were almost too big for anyone to take in.

The pain in her tight shoulders and wrinkled forehead stabbed at him. "I wish there was something I could do," he said. "I wish I could've protected you from hearing it."

"Wait," she said. "How long have you known?"

"That part of it, I've known for sure since Mom died six months ago."

She tilted her head to one side. "So you knew that…"

"I knew that my mother had an affair with a guest, and I later learned, when she was dying, that Kitty was the product of that affair."

"But how do you know it was my dad? Surely it wasn't my dad. He wouldn't…" She stared at the postcards on the table between them, then looked away.

He took a sip of lukewarm coffee. "When you mentioned the places where your family lived when you were a kid, the list rang a bell. Mom had shown me these—" He picked up the postcards, then put them down again. "She'd shown me the postcards that Kitty's father had written to her, keeping her updated about where he was."

Her eyes filled with tears. She stared at the postcards. Jake could see it becoming real to her.

Keep going. Get it over with.

"Apparently, he wanted her to know because he thought Kitty might share something genetic and need medical information. Anyway, when I heard where and how you grew up, when the places sounded so familiar, I dug up the postcards and looked at them. And then…"

Her throat worked. She grabbed a napkin from the holder on the table and dabbed at her eyes. "Go on," she rasped out.

"Remember when I asked to see your albums? That's when I realized for sure that the man in question was your father. I recognized him."

Her eyes narrowed, looking into his. Then she stared down at the table, running her finger around and around the circle of condensation from her glass. "You pretended you just wanted to see my family pictures because you were interested in my life. And then, when you figured out that my dad was the one, you didn't tell me."

Jake's stomach churned. She was getting angry at him.

He tried to explain his thinking. "I hoped I could protect you, the way I've tried to protect Kitty and my dad from this information. That was my mother's request, that I keep it to myself. She didn't think either of them was strong enough to handle it."

"So wait," she said, looking up at him again. "You said… Kitty is my sister? My half sister?"

He nodded. "I mean, I don't have a DNA test. But that's what Mom believed. And when you mentioned your dad being colorblind… Mason is, too. That's genetic. So I put it all together."

She was quiet. He could almost see the wheels turning in her head as she took it all in.

Maybe this wasn't going to be as bad as he'd feared. Maybe she wouldn't blame Jake. Maybe she wouldn't be all that upset about her image of her father being tarnished. On some level, she must have known what he was like.

Maybe, most importantly, she'd be willing to keep the news from Kitty and Dad.

She pushed back her chair with a loud scrape and stood. "So all this has been going through your mind for the past three weeks, and you didn't see fit to tell me about it?"

"Like I said, I wanted to protect you. I didn't want you to be disillusioned about your dad."

"Well, guess what." She propped both hands on her hips. "I *am* disillusioned about him. And I'm disillusioned about you, too. I thought we were getting close, becoming friends. Maybe more. But you don't keep big secrets from your friends."

"I—"

"Did you think I was a child who couldn't be told the truth?" she interrupted. "For that matter, is that what you think of your sister? And your dad? How patronizing is that?"

Anger flashed up in him. He'd been trying to do the right thing.

Just as quickly, the anger died. She was probably right. "I don't know, maybe I screwed up. I'm prone to it."

She rolled her eyes. "Don't go for pity. This is on you, this decision you made to keep something important from me."

"That's why I backed off," he said. He felt defensive, knew he was acting defensive. "It didn't seem right for me to be keeping that from you and also, well, be getting closer." Even as he said it, he could barely remember why he'd thought keeping the secret and backing off would be the better option than sharing the truth with her right away. Just his instinct to keep things to himself, he guessed. That was something his wife had repeatedly complained about. She'd called him a closed, locked book.

She blew out a breath, looked up at the ceiling. "Who all knows?"

"No one but me and Pastor Kevin."

She sank back into her chair. “What kind of woman was your mom? What kind of man was my dad?” She laid her head down on the table.

Jake had never been the best at dealing with emotions, his own or those of other people. “Summer?”

She didn’t answer. Didn’t move.

Was she crying? Praying? Had she passed out?

He walked around the table and touched her shoulder. “I want to help you with this,” he said. “I’m sorry it came out this way. And I’m sorry I didn’t tell you right away.”

She pushed his hand away. “Get out of here.”

“It doesn’t have to change anything, Summer. I really care about you, and I was hoping we could—”

“Get out.” She glared at him with cold, furious eyes. “I can’t stand the sight of you.”

Jake reeled back. Could her feelings about him really change that quickly? He was the same person he’d always been, but now suddenly, she couldn’t stand the sight of him?

Then resignation swept over him like a blanket, covering and muffling everything.

Of course he’d done something to ruin her liking of him. It was just what he’d done with his wife: his very personality, his nature, had ended up repelling her.

If he were a better man, he could have talked it out with Summer, explained himself until she understood, defended his choices.

But he was a man who was a poor communicator and who made bad choices. It was who he was. His wife had made that very, very clear. Summer’s slumped shoulders and angry, tear-filled eyes were just more evidence of what he’d already known.

He could give her this, at least: he could do what she’d requested. He could leave her alone. He turned and left the kitchen, feeling a hundred years old, every joint aching, muscles too weak to straighten his shoulders.

He'd hurt Summer, and badly. Possibly, his dad and his sister would get hurt, too, as a result of what Summer had discovered.

He'd failed them all, just like he'd failed his wife and child.

He walked to his suite, slowly, knowing it would be a long and sleepless night.

The day after learning the truth about her father, Summer couldn't put on enough makeup to hide the puffy dark circles under her eyes.

She'd lain awake most of the night, thinking about what she'd heard.

Her father had been intimate with Jake's mother. Out of that intimacy had come Kitty.

It seemed too outlandish to be true. She'd drifted off to sleep, had awakened thinking it was all a bad dream, and then remembered the postcards in her father's handwriting.

It was a beautiful May Sunday. Summer could see that objectively, see the green lawns and the spring flowers on the way to church, feel the fresh breeze blowing through the church windows, hear the birds singing outside. But she couldn't enjoy the beauty of spring. She couldn't feel happy.

As the service went on around her, she tried to focus on her goal: to process what she'd heard, figure out whether she could stay on at the guesthouse and in River Haven, and then, whatever her decision, get the kids on board.

She was furious that Jake had concealed this damaging information from her these past weeks. How demeaning could you get? He might think he was trying to protect her, but she was an adult, a mother with two kids who'd been through a lot in her twenty-eight years. She could handle the truth. The fact that he didn't see her strength, that he'd hidden something so big, was outrageous.

Hearing the peaceful music of the offertory around her, she tried to let her anger go. Took deep breaths.

But without her anger, she just felt devastated. How could her dad have done this, kept it a secret, betrayed her mother?

Did *all* men betray their families?

Numbly, she dug in her purse and pulled out a couple of bills for the offering plate. Even that made her think of her father. On the occasions when they'd gone to church, he had always dropped a fifty- or hundred-dollar bill in the plate. When, as a kid, she'd asked him why, he'd laughed and said he needed all the help with God that he could get. At which point her mother would turn to Summer and tell her that Dad was just a generous person.

Which was true. He had been quick to pick up the tab in a restaurant or to drop money in a beggar's cup.

All that time, he'd been a cheater. Just like Chuck had been.

Thinking of her dad in that light made her want to break down and weep.

She looked down the pew at Jake, instead. He sat watching and listening to the minister's sermon, appearing interested. Pious, even.

Who did he think he was, the boss of the world? Deciding what she could know and what she couldn't? What his sister and dad could know? He was a liar, too, hiding the truth, thinking himself too good to have to be honest, thinking he knew it all.

She looked down at her knees, sticking out from beneath her old sundress, scabbed from a fall she'd taken playing catch with Wyatt. Jake had played, too. He'd helped her up and gotten her antibiotic ointment and oversized bandages.

Thinking of him as an all-around horrible person wasn't fair, she could see that. His offense wasn't anywhere near the level of Chuck's, nor her father's. But why did *she* have to be the fair one all the time, the bigger person, overlooking mistreatment, forgiving people?

She breathed in the smell of candles and spring air. The music swelled up for the closing hymn, and she stood, mechanically. She checked on Wyatt, who was sitting down the pew toward Jake, next to Mason and Kitty.

Being hard and unforgiving was a wrong attitude to have in church, but it was real. It was how she felt.

So what was she supposed to do? Stay with Jake in his guesthouse full of lies, or start over somewhere else?

The question ate at her as the service ended, as she walked out of the church, as she greeted people she hadn't known a month ago, but who now felt like friends. Rylee and Wyatt ran around on the church lawn, playing with new friends of their own.

She accepted a glass of lemonade and stood at the edge of the sociable crowd.

Could she and the kids stay somewhere else in River Haven, continue attending the same church, stay at the same school for Wyatt and preschool for Rylee?

It would be a compromise. It would keep the kids in this place that was working so well for them while being bearable for her. It would keep the truth from coming out to Kitty and Mr. Wright, keep them, at least, from being hurt. She didn't think that was right, not really. They should know the truth about their family. But that wasn't her decision nor her business.

She'd have to find a new job, once the Mother's Day Open House was over. She couldn't abandon that, not at this late date, but she couldn't bear working with Jake much longer. First a new place to live, and then a new job.

Back to where they'd started. Homeless again.

It made her realize anew how good they'd had it, with a job and a ready-made place to live.

Unfortunately, that was all ruined.

She saw Jake, walking away from the church with Kitty and Mason and Mr. Wright. Couldn't take her eyes off him. That hurt most of all. She'd gotten her hopes up, stupidly, about the potential connection between them. Now, it wouldn't go forward.

Wyatt ran to her, Rylee following as fast as her little legs would carry her, trying to keep up. He pointed at the departing figures of the Wright family. "Come on, Mom, they're leaving. Let's go!"

She needed to let them know about her decision to leave the guesthouse, but that wouldn't happen if they slipped into their Sunday routine of hanging out with the Wrights at the guesthouse. "I have an idea," she said, injecting enthusiasm she didn't feel into her voice. "Let's go out to brunch at that pancake house on the highway." Her kids loved pancakes. Maybe getting fancy ones at a restaurant would ease them into accepting the new plan.

"I don't wanna sit at a restaurant," Wyatt said. "Mason and me are gonna go fishing."

"And I don't wanna go without Mr. Grandpa," Rylee said, pointing toward the disappearing figures of the Wrights.

When had Rylee started calling Mr. Wright Grandpa?

It made her realize how deeply involved the two of them were at the guesthouse. Leaving would be painful. But she couldn't let them stay longer. Couldn't let their attachment deepen any more.

Still, she needed to watch her funds if she was going to

quit the guesthouse job soon. So, rather than spending the money for a brunch they'd just sulk through, she agreed to go back to the guesthouse. "We'll have some sandwiches and then a talk," she said, but they were already running down the sidewalk and didn't seem to hear.

The talk didn't go well.

Summer took the kids out onto the deck, hoping the sunshine would bring cheer to what she was saying. But it turned out they weren't the only ones seeking a boost outdoors.

Jake was working on the flower beds around the guesthouse, weeding and planting flowers. It was what they'd discussed, making the place look great for the upcoming open house. But his demeanor was subdued, his expression closed.

Mr. Wright seemed to sense that things weren't okay, too. He sat on a bench at the far end of the guesthouse's large deck, watching Jake work, but not sharing his usual humorous advice.

Summer sat the kids down at their end of the deck, well out of earshot of the two men. "We're going to move out of the guesthouse," she told them. "We'll find a place of our own where you can each have your own bedroom!"

Both kids immediately shook their heads.

"I don't want to move," Wyatt said flatly.

"I like sleeping in the bedroom with you, Mommy," Rylee said.

Realizing she wasn't going to sell them on the idea that another place would be better, she settled on what they *would* think was positive. "We can stay in River Haven, or really close by," she said. "You can still go to your same schools. We can go to the same church."

"I wanna stay *here*," Rylee said, her lower lip sticking out.

"Me, too." Wyatt crossed his arms. "I like being next door to Mason."

"You can visit your friends a lot," Summer said. The truth was, this was a really small town. There'd be no getting away from the Wrights. "We'll still be close by, but we need to find a place of our own."

Rylee started to cry. "I don't wanna leave Mr. Grandpa! And my kitties!"

With superb bad timing, Mr. Wright walked back into the house with his coffee cup, which brought him close enough for Rylee to notice. She ran to him. "Mommy says we have to move away!" She wrapped herself around his leg like a little monkey.

Wyatt slumped down in his chair, his face wearing the same sulky expression he'd had when they'd arrived.

"Now, honey," Mr. Wright said to Rylee, "are you sure you've got that right?"

"Come tell Mommy no!" Rylee commanded. She let go of his leg, grabbed his hand and tugged him toward Summer.

The old man looked at her, head tilted to one side. "You're leaving?"

"I'll keep working on the Mother's Day Open House," Summer reassured him. "But, yeah, we're going to move out."

He nodded once, looked down at Rylee, and ran a weathered hand over her hair. When he looked up at Summer, his eyes were suspiciously shiny. "I'm sorry to hear that," he said with a little catch in his voice. "These kiddos—all of you, really—have brought this place back to life."

He didn't ask why they were leaving. His was a polite generation that didn't pry. But she could see the questions in his eyes, and the betrayal, too.

"It's been wonderful, and you've been a generous host, but

it's time for us to find our own place," she said firmly. "Is the Sunday paper inside? I'd like to take a look at the classified ads, see what rentals I can find." She'd look at jobs, too. River Haven was an old-fashioned enough town that a lot of people still used the newspaper rather than posting apartments or job openings online.

"Yes, it's in the kitchen," Mr. Wright said. He looked down at Rylee, who was still holding his hand. "You go play, little lady. It's time for this old man to take a nap." He headed inside, his shoulders stooped.

"I don't wanna play," Rylee wailed.

"I'm going fishing, away from *you,*" Wyatt practically snarled, pointing at Summer. He ran off the deck toward the river, where Mason had already thrown his fishing line in the water.

Rylee ran after him.

Summer felt like crying, too. Especially when she saw that Jake had moved closer with his bushel basket and weeding tools.

She liked seeing him this way, working around the house on a Sunday afternoon. Liked the feeling of family.

But what was family, anyway? Her experience with family was looking worse and worse. Family seemed like a place where lies were told, hopes were dashed and dreams were punctured and destroyed.

She leaned back in her chair, letting her head fall back, looking up at the sky. She felt as limp as a weed from Jake's stack, wilting in the bushel basket.

Get it together. You're a mom, you can't fall apart.

A better person would stand up and walk over to Jake and tell him in a calm, factual way that she was moving out and giving notice. That she'd stay and help with the open house, but that he'd need to find someone else to fill the job, after that.

She couldn't do it.

Summer was sick to death of pretending calm maturity during conversations that were gutting her. She'd had enough of that for a lifetime, talking to Chuck, trying to get him to explain himself and stick around for the kids.

And she was exhausted from the miserable conversation she'd just had with the kids. She'd made them so unhappy. Undoubtedly, she'd undone some of the progress they'd made during their time here.

Was it a mistake to move away? And yet, how could she stay?

A blue jay landed on the deck railing and scolded her. Well, she deserved it. It was no more harsh and raucous than her own inner voice, scolding herself.

Chapter Fourteen

Jake worked hard on the flower beds surrounding the guesthouse all Sunday afternoon and into the evening, foregoing dinner, tilling the soil better than it had ever been tilled before, spreading mulch.

There was no question about it: he was punishing himself. All the problems in the guesthouse—Dad's sadness, the kids' upset, Summer's closed-off coldness—were due to his own action of keeping the truth to himself.

He'd just loaded his tools into the wheelbarrow, finally ready to call it a day, when Kitty pulled into the driveway between the guesthouse and her place.

"I'm home with the haul, come help," she called through the open driver's-side window. She got out and opened the hatch, revealing boxes and bags of supplies from her monthly trip to the warehouse store.

"Be right there." He pushed the wheelbarrow into the shed and then headed over to Kitty's vehicle.

Man, he wished he could talk to her about the whole situation. Kitty would get it. She'd been his fan, at his side and on his side, since the day she was born. Even when he screwed up, she loved him.

Except that the thing he wanted to discuss with her would

be a bombshell for her, too. Would she react as badly as Summer had?

He carried a heavy box full of canned goods into the guesthouse kitchen and came back for a second load. “Where’s Mason? He usually helps.”

Kitty pointed down toward the river. Mason sat on the bank, talking with Wyatt. Rylee was running away from them, toward Juniper, who was swinging on her playset. Rylee spoke to the other little girl and then the two of them ran back toward Wyatt and Mason. To Jake’s surprise, the boys seemed to welcome the younger girls rather than telling them to get lost.

“Mason said Summer and her kids are moving out,” Kitty said as she lifted a couple of bags. “Is it true?”

He hoisted another box and followed her inside, carrying it. “Yeah. That’s what Dad told me. He’s bummed out.” Jake’s whole motivation for keeping the secret had been to protect people—Dad, Kitty and then Summer—but it hadn’t worked. Dad had gotten hurt already, and he didn’t even know the truth.

“I’m sure. He’s gotten real attached to them, especially Rylee.” She set down her bags, then nodded toward the kitchen island. “Put the box over there. Do you know why they’re leaving?”

Jake didn’t have it in him to pretend. “Yeah. Pretty sure I do.”

“Is she leaving us in the lurch about the open house?”

Jake couldn’t even remember what she’d said about that, if anything. “Not sure.”

They walked back to the car and started unloading Kitty’s part of the haul. “The kids will be so sad.” She pointed toward the foursome on the riverbank, uncharacteristically sitting still rather than running around. "They all get along so well."

They carried in the rest of the supplies in silence, but Jake's mind raced with self-accusation. He'd failed to protect anyone. He'd thought he could do it by keeping his knowledge a secret, but there had been a big price to pay when the truth came out. Had he been wrong about his approach after all?

After they'd finished, Jake looked at Kitty. She stood leaning back against the sink, arms crossed, one eyebrow raised.

He *wanted* to talk to her about the whole thing. Summer's reaction had made him realize that it was wrong to keep such important information from an adult. And the minister had said secrets were toxic. "Sit down," he said for the second time in two days.

He sat opposite his sister, took a deep breath and told her the truth about her father.

"Wait, *what?*" she said when he was finished. "You mean Summer's dad is actually my father? Mom *did* that?"

"Yeah. It's a lot." He blew out a sigh. "I'm sorry I didn't tell you before, right after Mom died and I knew the whole truth. I should have."

She sat a minute, forehead wrinkled. Then she reached across the table and smacked his arm, lightly. "Yes, you should have told me! Come on, Jake, stop living in the past. Women can actually handle real life. In fact, we handle a lot more real life than we're given credit for."

"You're right. I was being boneheaded. And it's not like I did anything useful with the information. You would have handled it all better than I did."

"Uh-huh. Did Mom tell you not to tell me?"

He nodded. "She thought, with all you were going through with the divorce, it would be too much."

She rolled her eyes, then sighed. "You could be right. Now, I feel like I'm just so jaded from big emotions that I can't even feel this." She frowned. "Wait. You and I are only half-siblings?"

"Biologically." He reached out and squeezed her hand. "Truth is, you're my sister all the way."

Her lips curved upward and she squeezed back. Then her eyes widened. "Summer is my half sister? I always wanted a sister!"

"She is," he said. "I don't think she's processed it yet, so maybe hold off on making a big deal out of it."

"Right." She sat for a moment, lost in thought. Then she shook her head rapidly, as if shaking her ruminations off. "Want some coffee?"

"That would be great."

She fixed him a cup of dark roast in her pod coffeemaker, then made a cup for herself. Obviously, she was thinking about what he'd told her, because her hands kept going still, and her expression kept changing, various emotions flashing across her face.

She sat down across from him and they both sipped coffee for a minute. "So Summer is upset?" she asked finally.

"Yeah. For me keeping it from her, that her dad was the one Mom had an affair with."

"How long did you know that?"

"Three weeks." He explained about the photo albums and the color blindness.

She whistled. "Wow. Mason actually inherited something from that dude."

"Yeah. Weird, huh?"

"Very." She frowned. "Summer's upset you kept it from her for *three weeks*? She's actually moving out because of it?"

"Seems that way."

"You kept it from me for a lot longer, you jerk." But her words had no heat in them.

"What about Dad?"

Jake turned his cup around and around in his hands. "We'll tell him later, I guess?" He looked up at her. "Let's think about what's best for him."

Suddenly, Kitty's face crumpled. "He's not my real dad." A tear ran down her face, then another.

He stood and circled the table to hug her from behind. "I'm sorry, sis." He grabbed a box of tissues and handed them to her.

She blew her nose and wiped her eyes. "Go sit down," she ordered. "Let me think." As Jake obeyed, she looked up at the ceiling and blew out a breath. "You know what? He *is* my dad. I don't care about this cheating guy who loved and left Mom."

Jake winced. "To be fair, I think Mom was a willing participant."

They sat for a few more minutes. The sun was half-down behind the trees across the river now, making a gorgeous show of orange and purple and gold through Kitty's big kitchen window.

"I'd better go get Mason in," Kitty said finally.

They both stood.

"So, whatever was happening between you and Summer is on the rocks for now?"

He nodded, swallowed hard. He couldn't pretend to be okay about it.

She put an arm around him as she headed toward the door, and he put his arm around her, comforted by the closeness. He couldn't ask for a better sister. She'd been right there with him in Mom's death and Dad's grief. And yeah, she was a little mad at him for keeping the truth to himself, but she seemed to understand that he'd been doing what he thought was right.

Outside, they both looked toward the river. Wyatt and Mason were throwing a football. The little girls must have gone inside. It was their bedtime. When he looked up toward the window of their suite, he could see Summer and Rylee moving around inside, blurry and indistinct through the curtain.

"When do you think she'll move?" Kitty asked.

"She asked Dad for the Sunday paper, to look at the classified ads. I think she's looking for places online, now. She's serious, and seems like she wants to get going fast on it." The thought of the guesthouse without Summer and the kids in it tightened his throat painfully. "It seems like she hates me," he managed to say.

"Oh, man." Kitty hugged him. "I'm sorry, brother. Just remember, you're not in this alone. I'm with you all the way. Not *half*way," she added with emphasis.

"Thanks," he said, meaning it. Having someone on his side, having Kitty articulate that so strongly even after he'd dropped a bombshell on her, meant a lot more than he would ever have thought.

Being strong and silent and unemotional might be his natural tendency, and the military and his male-dominated career choice had pushed him further in that direction. But he was starting to realize that there were drawbacks to keeping everything to himself. And benefits to letting people in.

On Monday afternoon, Summer stood in a living room on the far side of River Haven. An anxious landlady hovered nearby.

Summer had put in her time working on the guesthouse today. She didn't want to slack on her job just because she was furious at one of her bosses, Jake, and felt guilty about the other, Mr. Wright. Or Mr. Grandpa, as Rylee insisted on calling him.

She couldn't say the Holiday Haven Guesthouse was truly ready for guests, not quite. But Jake and Kitty and Mr. Wright could finish it, and then they could find someone to fulfill the role of managing it, the role Summer had been supposed to play.

The Mother's Day Open House was coming up this weekend, and Summer intended to fulfill her commitment of pulling that off. She could handle working with Jake for that long. She could. She'd even texted with him today when she'd had a question only he could answer, a terse text that had taken her twenty minutes to compose. He'd answered, and that was that. None of the banter they usually shared via text, when he was working at his shop and she was working at the guesthouse.

She did a 360 turn, trying to imagine herself and the kids living here. It was nice, really. Half a duplex, with a fenced backyard and three bedrooms. The landlady was eager to rent it to her right away, because her former tenants had left without notice at the end of April.

"I live in the other half, but I don't bother the tenants if they don't bother me," the landlady told her. "It's walking distance to the elementary school and the park. And there's a grocery store just on the next block."

Summer already knew the logistics. The apartment was almost the same distance from the middle of town that the guesthouse was, just in the opposite direction. Which meant that Wyatt and Rylee could technically walk to the guesthouse from here, although not without supervision.

"I hope you'll take it," the landlady said. "I have someone else who's interested, but it's three young men, and I'm worried about noise and partying."

"My kids aren't quiet," Summer warned her.

The woman waved a hand. "I'm not worried about the noise kids make. I like little ones. Used to be a teacher."

Summer walked into the kitchen and took a look around. It would be nice to have her own kitchen rather than having to share with Jake and Mr. Wright, she told herself firmly. Nice, too, to have more space to spread out.

"I *think* I'll take it," she said. "I just need to give it a little more thought, but if we do move in, it would probably be this week. Can I let you know later tonight?"

"Of course, dear. I know it's complicated with little ones."

Summer looked around a little more and then drove home slowly. As she passed the school, she thought of her son, and dread seized her. She'd have to talk Wyatt into the move. Rylee would follow Wyatt's lead.

She walked into the guesthouse. It was unusually quiet. Mr. Wright wasn't in his usual chair. Then she remembered that it was Monday, the day he'd started meeting with afternoon coffee buddies. She was relieved that he'd still gone, rather than sitting around the house being sad. He was going to be fine when they moved away, just fine.

Rylee was at a playdate with Gemma's daughter. But Wyatt should be here. Maybe he was doing homework upstairs. "Wyatt?" she called.

No answer. Maybe Wyatt was over at Gemma's. Or at Mason's, or down by the river.

She walked across the lawn to Gemma's place and knocked on the door.

Gemma looked confused. "Rylee went off with Wyatt a little while ago," she said. "Didn't you send him?"

"No. I just got home."

"I'm sorry. Since you usually let Wyatt take her, I figured it was okay. They're not at the guesthouse?"

"No." Worry tugged at Summer.

"Want me to come help look for them? They have to be close by."

Summer could see that Gemma had been working at her computer. Juniper lay on the couch, watching a kids' show on TV. "They must be at Kitty's place," she said. "I'll find them. No worries."

But no one was home at Kitty's place. Summer's stomach tightened and her heart raced out of control. Her kids were missing.

Unless…could they be at the auto shop? Even though they weren't allowed to go there unless specifically invited by Jake?

Jake. If they weren't with him, he would help her find them. She speed walked from Kitty's house to the shop and rushed inside.

Chapter Fifteen

Just from the way Summer burst through the door, letting it bang behind her, Jake knew something was wrong.

She looked around, wide eyes scanning the shop. "Wyatt? Rylee?"

Jake grabbed a rag and walked over to her, wiping his hands. "What's happened?"

"I can't find them! They're gone! Rylee and Wyatt!"

The panic in her voice made him take a deep breath and relax his shoulders. It had always been that way with him. In emergencies, he went into soldier mode, tamping down any emotions of his own that wanted to rear up.

"Are they here?" She walked around the shop, her movements jerky, eyes wild as she looked behind stacks of tires and beneath cars awaiting work.

"They're not here." He'd been alone in the shop today and would have seen and heard them. "Where'd you see them last?"

"Wyatt should have gotten off the school bus an hour ago, but I forgot your dad wouldn't be home. Wyatt went and got Rylee from Gemma's, and they're gone!"

"Settle. Take a breath. They can't have gone far." His brain clicked through the possibilities. "Let's check by the river first."

He didn't want to say it, but that was the riskiest place. When she gasped, her hand flying to her mouth, he knew she understood.

They rushed down together, both of them jogging. When they got to the riverbank and saw nothing out of the ordinary, they split ways, Jake going to the right toward Kitty's side of the property, Summer to the left toward Gemma's.

A moment later, they met at the middle again, at the dock below the guesthouse. "No sign of them," she said. "Do you think…" She trailed off, looking out at the water, biting her lip. She was hanging on by a thread, that was obvious.

"The boat isn't gone," he pointed out, scanning the muddy bank, "and there are no footprints. They're not here."

He turned away from the river, looking up at the guesthouse and surrounding yards. There were so many places a kid could go.

"Come *on,*" she exclaimed, starting toward the guesthouse. "Wyatt! Rylee!"

He followed, thinking fast. "Someone needs to search through the guesthouse. I'll call Dad and he can do that, he knows every nook and cranny. We'll divide the outdoors into segments. Kitty will help." He pulled out his phone.

Summer was breathing so hard that it looked like she might hyperventilate. He put a hand on her shoulder. *If someone's panicking, give them a job,* he remembered his CO saying. "Call Gemma and see if she'll drive around searching the roads. She can take Juniper with her." He was scanning the area for movement but saw none.

Moments later, he'd gotten through to his father, who was on his way home. Gemma's car was backing out of her driveway; she tooted the horn and waved and then drove slowly down the road. Kitty had been waiting to pick up Mason from an after-school activity. She grimly agreed to grill him and find out what he knew.

"Why would the kids run?" he asked Summer as he knelt to search the bushes beside the deck.

Summer was up above him on the deck, searching under chairs and tables and benches. "They're angry because I told them we have to move," she said. "It's my fault."

"Don't go there. No time for guilt." He barked it out like an order, but she didn't get upset. She just gulped and nodded.

Jake had half expected to find the kids within a couple of minutes, but that wasn't happening. He pictured little Rylee, barely more than a toddler. And Wyatt, while taller and lankier, was only ten. His gut twisted.

"Jake." Summer dropped to her knees on the deck, breathing hard. "What if someone took them?"

"Very unlikely." He spoke with more confidence than he felt. "It's River Haven. People notice strangers and look out for each other." Then a disturbing possibility entered his mind. "What about their father? Is he the type who'd abduct his own kids?"

Her eyes widened and she shook her head back and forth, slowly. "No. No, I don't think so. He knows I'll let him see them. But… I can call him if it comes to that."

She was reluctant, he could see that. Understandably, she didn't want to rouse the man with questions about where the kids were, which might call her own competence as a parent into question. "We'll hunt for half an hour. If we don't find them in that amount of time, we'll go wider. The pastor can get some of the church people involved, and we can contact their dad. And the state police."

She went pale.

"You take that side of the guesthouse," he said, pointing, "and I'll take this one. We'll meet out front."

"What's that?" she asked, rushing across the deck toward what looked like a pile of clothes.

He followed her. It was Wyatt's jacket and Rylee's stuffed bear.

"Rylee will be upset without her bear," she said, her voice leaning toward hysteria.

He put a hand on both her shoulders. "I've seen her without it lots of times," he said sternly. "She'll be okay. We can't afford for you to panic now. Go search your side." He pointed, then headed toward the side of the guesthouse he'd said he'd search.

As they met in the front, Jake's father's car squealed up with a spray of gravel. "I'll search inside," he said. "I know every hiding place. We'll find them, don't worry."

Dad hurried inside.

"Train tracks next," Jake ordered.

Summer gulped and nodded.

Jake's stomach twisted harder. He'd come to care for those kids, a lot, and the thought of them out here somewhere, scared, was almost more than he could handle. He pushed the images out of his mind. He had to help Summer, comfort her and help her find her kids. He had to be the strong one.

Gemma drove up slowly and lowered her window. "I've looked on all the roads they could travel within half a mile," she said. "Nothing."

Then Kitty's car squealed into the driveway. She jumped out and opened the back door. "Get out here and tell them," she ordered Mason.

He was crying. "I told them they'd get in trouble," he said.

"Where are they, honey?" Summer knelt in front of the boy, her voice gentler than Jake could have managed.

"They could be in the attic," Mason said.

Summer stood.

Jake's father had come out and heard what Mason said. "Not there," he said. "I checked."

"Then, under the shed where the kittens are. That was the backup plan."

They all rushed out to the shed. Jake found a loose section of crisscross trellis and pulled it back, and Summer crawled in without a second's hesitation. "Rylee? Wyatt?"

"Mommy!" Rylee's voice was the sweetest sound Jake had ever heard.

There were shuffling noises, and then Summer scooted back out with Rylee in her arms. Wyatt trailed behind. Both faces were tearstained.

Quickly, Jake knelt and examined Wyatt, then did a visual scan of Rylee, who wouldn't let go of her mother. "You kids okay?" he asked, hearing the gruffness in his own voice. It was that or bust out bawling, he was so relieved.

"We're okay, but *she* got scared," Wyatt said.

Minutes later, they were all on the deck of the guesthouse, and the kids were explaining their wacky plan. "We were gonna hide until Mom gave up and moved away without us," Wyatt said. "Mason was gonna bring us food."

"And Mr. Grandpa would have helped," Rylee said. She slid out of Summer's lap and went to stand next to Jake's father. "You would have helped us, right?"

Dad just ran a hand over her hair and shook his head. His eyes looked a little teary. "You gave us quite a scare," he said. "Why did you do that?"

"Cuz we don't want to leave," she said, leaning against him.

"Oh, man." Summer had her arm around Wyatt, now. "You kids know better than to pull a stunt like that."

"Will we have a punishment?" Wyatt asked.

Summer nodded. "You sure will. And you have to promise never to run away or hide again."

"We won't, Mommy," Rylee said. "I got too scared."

Wyatt just nodded, but Jake could see from the expression on his face that he was taking his mother's words seriously.

Summer looked around at the rest of them. "Thank you all, so much. I was flipping out and you all dropped everything to help." She looked at Jake with a smile that seemed especially warm.

He wanted to ask her if she still planned to move out. If she was still angry at him. But he didn't have the emotional energy, and he was pretty sure she didn't, either.

Dad had no such qualms. He leaned toward Summer and spoke to her, low, but Jake could hear what he said. "You're right to punish them, of course," he said, "but you might want to listen to them, too. They gave you a pretty big message today."

She nodded, her eyes shiny with tears. "That's true," she said. "We're going to have a big talk, once we've all settled down."

Jake glanced over at Kitty and found that she was watching him. "We need to have a talk, too, and sooner rather than later," she said. She pointed in a circle toward Jake, herself and their father.

Jake swallowed hard and nodded. "You're right," he said. "Lots of talking to do."

Twenty-four hours later, Summer was starting to recover from the terror of Monday night.

She dug through her shirts, looking for something a little dressier than her usual practical T-shirts. She pulled out a silky royal blue top and then tossed it aside. Maybe the black.

A wardrobe upgrade was in order, just as soon as she got

a little ahead financially. In fact, she might check out an online thrift shop even sooner.

She glanced over at Rylee, who was playing with her dolls. Two were hiding behind a chair, and the other two were searching and calling for them.

Amazing how kids processed things through play, got it all worked out in their own heads.

Summer intended to get it worked out in her head, too. That was why she'd agreed to go out with Kitty and Gemma tonight. She hoped her new friends—one of them a recently discovered sister—would help her work through her complicated feelings about whether to stay in the guesthouse or move on.

She settled on a red shirt and pulled it over her head, then studied herself in the mirror. If she ever went out with Jake, maybe she'd wear this.

Not that she intended to do that. Not that he'd even want to.

She was torn between being ashamed of the way she'd blamed him for keeping information away from her and impressed with how capably he'd managed the search for Rylee and Wyatt. He'd been so helpful, had stepped up without even a second's hesitation even though she'd been giving him the silent treatment for the previous two days.

On her way to the bathroom to add a little makeup, she stopped to look into Wyatt's bedroom. He was there, playing with the tiny green army figures Mr. Wright had dug out of the attic for him. As she watched, Wyatt crumpled up a piece of paper and dropped it on his formation of soldiers, making the appropriate whistling sound and then yelling "boom!" when the paper landed.

She smiled and went on into the bathroom. Boys would be boys.

Kids would be kids. Her two had come up with a silly plan to try to stay in the guesthouse. They'd sincerely thought that they could hide for days, until she gave up and moved without them.

Of course, that was ridiculous. But it spoke to how much they wanted to stay.

And she needed to listen, like Mr. Wright had said. Kids had an innate wisdom, a keen sense of what was a safe place and what wasn't. They knew what was important, and it wasn't about some ancient history between her dad and Jake's mom. What was important was now.

She stroked on mascara, added lipstick and called it good enough. Then she went out into the living room where Rylee was lecturing her dolls.

"Don't you dare hide ever again!" Rylee scolded, her voice much sterner than Summer's had been when she'd scolded Rylee and Wyatt.

"Kids, come over here on the couch, both of you. Wyatt, that means you, too."

There was none of the usual foot-dragging. Within a few seconds, both kids were on the couch, Wyatt on one side and Rylee on the other. They were affected by what had happened, too. They'd been scared in that dark space under the shed.

"I want to hear from you," she said, an arm around each of them. "Can you explain to me why you hid yesterday? Why you want to stay here so much?"

Wyatt spoke up immediately. "We told you, we like living here. Our friends are right next door."

"'Zactly my same age," Rylee contributed.

Wyatt reached across Summer to high-five his sister. "Yeah! Mason is almost my age, and Juniper is almost

Rylee's age." He looked up at Summer. "Also, we can help Mr. Jake in his shop."

Summer wasn't sure the help they provided Jake would actually be helpful. But she also knew Jake wouldn't be mean about booting them out when he had to work.

"We can help Mr. Grandpa," Rylee contributed. "He gets lonely."

Summer swallowed hard. Truer words were never spoken. Mr. Wright *did* get lonely, and the bond he'd developed with her kids had helped him feel more connected. Moreover, her kids needed a grandpa, and he'd stepped kindly and willingly into the role.

She tried to push back a little without stopping them from confiding in her. "Don't you want us to have our own house and yard? We can't live in this little suite forever."

"Why not?" Wyatt asked. "We like it here. And it's cheaper. And Mr. Jake can fix our van when it breaks."

No one could argue like a ten-year-old. "Places like this are made just for vacations. And once it's all fixed up and people start coming to stay, we would have to be extra quiet. Maybe even give up this suite so paying guests could stay."

"We could sleep on the sofa," Rylee said. "While there were guests here."

"I'd sleep on the floor!" Wyatt frowned. "Or if we can't stay here, then we should get a house on this street."

There was a tap on the door. "Are you ready?" Kitty called. "Jake and Dad are grilling hot dogs for you kids."

"Yeah!" Wyatt scrambled off the couch.

"Not so fast, kiddos." Summer went to the door and stood in front of it blocking their exit. Then she gave them each a tight hug. "I'm going to think about what you said. Love you bunches."

"Love you too, Mom." Wyatt opened the door and pushed past Kitty to clatter down the steps.

"Bye, Mommy," Rylee said. "Hi, Miss Kitty." Then she scurried after her brother.

Summer watched them, her throat tightening again. They were everything to her.

"Nice to see how well they get along," Kitty said. "I wish Mason had a little sister." She looked a little teary, too, and Summer resolved to ask Kitty about her future hopes, when the time was right.

"You look pretty," she said to Kitty. She wanted to make her feel better, but it was true. Kitty's short jeans skirt and purple T-shirt looked festive and fun.

"Thanks. Now, come on." Kitty grabbed Summer's arm. "Gemma's going out to start the car. Let's git while the gittin's good!"

Twenty minutes later, they were at a Mexican restaurant in a nearby town. The parking lot was nearly full, and loud music came from the outdoor patio.

Summer smacked herself lightly in the head. "It's Cinco de Mayo! That's why half the town is here!"

"I forgot too, until Gemma reminded me," Kitty said.

Gemma grabbed them both by the arm. "It's party time!" She started waving her hands in time to the music, and they all danced their way into the restaurant, laughing.

Inside, the place was colorful with decorations. Bright tiles lined the floor, and the chairs were painted in red and blue and green designs. Most of the tables were full of families, couples and friend groups, everyone talking and laughing and clearly having a good time.

"Thank you for this," Summer said as they slid into one of the last open booths. "I needed it."

"Don't we all." Gemma turned to the waiter who'd just

approached them. “We’re celebrating. Any chance you can make us some nonalcoholic margaritas?”

“Of course,” he said, smiling at them. “You ladies are up on the latest trend.”

“Who knew?” Kitty said.

“Not me, but I’m all in.” Summer stretched her back and rolled her tight shoulders. When was the last time she’d enjoyed a night out with girlfriends? It had been rare even when she’d been with Chuck, because he traveled so much and the kids were small. Neither of them had had family who could take the kids for an evening, giving them a break.

Surprisingly, in her few weeks in River Haven, she’d developed a better support system than she’d ever had in the city.

Their drinks arrived in big glasses with salt around the rims. They ordered—tacos for Gemma, and enchilada plates for Summer and Kitty—and then sipped their margaritas. The taste was frosty and tart and refreshing.

“You’re probably wondering why we wanted to go out,” Kitty said.

“Just for fun, right?” Summer took another sip.

“That’s right,” Gemma said, “but we also wanted to talk. See how you were doing about what happened yesterday. That was awful.”

Summer nodded, closing her eyes for a second. “Some of the worst moments of my life,” she said. “I can’t believe they did that.”

“Did they explain more about why?” Kitty asked.

So Summer told them about her conversation with Wyatt and Rylee.

Both women shook their heads.

“Kids,” Gemma said. “Never a dull moment.”

“They want to stay in the guesthouse. Their logic was

a little wacky, but their goal was crystal clear." Summer reached across the table and squeezed the other women's hands. "Thank you both for helping. It meant everything."

"Of course," Gemma said.

"We know you'd do the same for us," Kitty added. "If you stay, that is."

Her words hung awkwardly in the air. Summer truly didn't know what to do. She'd held off the landlord of the other place, but she had to make a decision by tomorrow.

Fortunately, their meals came, sparing Summer from more questions. They all dug in. Summer's enchiladas were delicious, hot and cheesy, and the beans and rice were full of flavor.

As they ate, they chatted about schools, both the preschool where Rylee and Gemma's daughter went, and the public elementary where Wyatt and Mason were in the same class. Kitty described fun opportunities to get involved, and Gemma chimed in with ideas about dance classes for little girls. Summer sensed that they were trying to sell her on staying in River Haven, but she didn't mind.

When they were groaningly full, Kitty raised her second margarita. "I have something to toast," she said, clinking the heavy glass with Summer's. "We're sisters!"

"He told you?" It was the one thing Summer was grateful for in this whole mixed-up business. She jumped up and bent over Kitty to hug her. "I always wanted a sister, and if I could have ordered one, you would be it!"

"Same!" Kitty hugged her back. "We're going to have so much fun. *If* you stay."

Right. That was the question. She wanted to stay in River Haven, but could she do it without the job at the guesthouse? On the other hand, could she stay at the guesthouse and work with Jake, knowing what had started up between them and how harshly she'd ended it?

As Summer sat down, Gemma tapped her glass to both of theirs. "I'm officially confused, but happy to celebrate."

Kitty looked at Summer and raised her eyebrows. Summer shrugged.

"You don't have to tell me," Gemma said quickly. "Believe me, I get it about keeping family business private."

That made Summer realize that she didn't know a whole lot about Gemma's background. She needed to at least open the door to that, since Gemma had been so kind and helpful about Summer's drama.

"I know you can keep this to yourself," Kitty said. "Do you want to tell her, Summer, or should I?"

In the end, they took turns telling the story of Summer's father and Kitty's mother that had resulted in their discovery that they were sisters. Gemma's eyes widened more and more as the story came out. "Wow," she said when they'd finished. "People sure are a mess sometimes, aren't they? And yet God works it all for good. You wouldn't be here," she added, pointing her straw at Kitty, "if your parents hadn't strayed from their partners."

"I guess," Kitty said, tilting her head to one side.

"And you," Gemma said to Summer, "you're mad at Jake because he didn't tell you as soon as he found out your dad was involved?"

Summer nodded. "I feel kind of stupid about it now," she said. "He was so great yesterday. I guess he was doing the best he could."

"He was. Even though the jerk kept the secret from me for like, months." Kitty rolled her eyes. "Protective big brother, that's Jake."

What Kitty said was true, Summer reflected. Jake was

a protector. That was his nature. In keeping the truth from her, he hadn't been out for personal gain; he'd just been trying to shield her from knowledge he thought would hurt her.

Kitty touched Summer's hand. "Is it really Jake you're mad at or is it your dad?" she asked. "Because I'm pretty mad at my mom. Both for what she did to Dad—and by Dad, I mean the father who actually stuck around and raised me—and for basically lying to me all those years."

Summer nodded slowly. "It's true," she said. "My dad was…complicated. I loved him more than anything. I spent my whole childhood trying to be cute enough and funny enough for him to stick around and love me back." Her throat closed up on the last words. She'd never articulated them before. Never admitted to herself that her father might have been wrong to want to spend his time with his friends instead of his family. Never considered that it was a parent's responsibility to love without conditions.

Kitty squeezed her hand. "I want to know more about him," she said. "Not now, but sometime. Maybe we can process some of this together, since we're basically in the same boat."

"Not to play armchair psychologist," Gemma said to Summer, "but you could also be transferring some of your anger at your husband onto Jake. Since your husband lied to you in such a big way."

Summer nodded. "You *should* be a psychologist. That makes sense. I'll have to think about it." She looked from Gemma to Summer and realized she felt closer to them than she'd ever felt to friends before. She'd gotten married so young and then had relied on Chuck for friendship that had turned out to be false. "I guess I was always trying to please my husband as well," she said. "When he left, I felt like I wasn't woman enough to keep him."

"No," Gemma said instantly. "This was *not* your fault."

"She's right," Kitty said.

But if it wasn't her fault, Summer thought as they paid their checks and headed back to River Haven, it certainly wasn't Jake's fault, either.

She had so much thinking to do. She was working through the events, not only of yesterday, but of her childhood and marriage as well. That would take time.

But she felt encouraged. With her new friends beside her, she was going to figure it all out.

Chapter Sixteen

On Wednesday morning, Jake and Kitty took their father out to breakfast at The Hungry Hubcap, Kitty having taken a day off from school for the occasion. They drove rather than walked, and jogged through the raindrops to the entrance. The front garage-type doors were usually open at this time of year, but today's rain meant the diner was closed up and steamy.

They got a table at the back, and since the main crowd of working people had already come and gone, they'd have privacy for their task.

Jake had had a day to think about all that had happened throughout the past week. The experience of hunting for the kids had sobered him. Made him realize how much he cared, not that it did him much good. Summer wasn't as cold as she'd been, but she wasn't exactly warm and bubbly toward him. He figured his chances with her had come and gone.

He shelved that thought to think about later. They all studied the menu, written up on a chalkboard behind the counter, and ordered their usual favorites: Dad and Jake went for the breakfast special: three eggs, bacon and hash browns. Kitty had a bowl of oatmeal with berries, saying she'd overeaten at the Mexican restaurant the night before.

Jake dreaded the conversation to come, but he knew they

had to have it. The events of Monday night had made him treasure his father for his wisdom, and with Kitty's ongoing lecturing, he'd realized that Dad deserved to know the truth, just like she had deserved it.

So their goal, today, was to tell Dad and help him manage. But it didn't work out as planned. Three of Dad's friends came over, and not knowing their plans for the breakfast, Dad invited the other men to sit down. Jake fidgeted through it, trying not to think about the time he was wasting listening to these old men jawboning.

"Right, Jake?" Kitty kicked him under the table, and he realized he hadn't been paying attention.

"Sorry, missed what you said," he apologized.

"Mr. Whittaker, here, was talking about setting his grandson up with Summer. Think she'd go for that?"

Jake snapped to attention. "You mean Walter? No. No, I don't think so."

"Why not?" the older man said. "It's true Walter lives in our basement, but he's a real good boy. Helps us out, and he's working on his GED. He's quit drinking and has a couple leads on jobs. When he saw her in church, he couldn't get over how pretty she is."

"That's true." Jake rubbed the back of his neck. Who was he to judge Mr. Whittaker's grandson? It wasn't like he was perfect, himself.

But the notion of Walter Whittaker taking Summer out gave him a bad case of indigestion. "Look, I've got to get back to the shop," he said.

During the short drive home, Dad and Kitty kept snickering. "Sticks in your craw a little bit, does it, son?" Dad asked. "You know, if you don't want someone else to snag Summer, you'd better ask her out yourself."

"She wouldn't go," he grouched, and headed out to the shop.

About 10:00 a.m., Kitty texted him. I'm bringing Dad out now. Can you talk?

He wiped his hands and texted back a thumbs-up. Why not? It wasn't as if he were getting any work done, anyway.

It was all swirling around him, the need to tell Dad, the confusion about Summer, the confusion about his own role in the world. If it wasn't to protect his family, then what was it?

Dad and Kitty came in on a gusty breeze that blew the door closed behind them. They sat down in the chairs in the shop's waiting area. Jake saw that the magazines on the end table were all more than a year old, something he'd never noticed because he never sat here, himself. The coffeemaker was kind of dirty from this angle, too. Jake wasn't the best at making things fancy. His customers didn't expect it.

"Kitty tells me you two have something to discuss with me," Dad said. He got up, poured himself a cup of stale coffee, took a sip and grimaced, then sat back down in the chair between theirs.

"Yeah." Jake took a deep breath and looked at Kitty.

She nodded encouragingly but didn't speak.

It was on Jake, then. He cleared his throat. "So, ah, Mom told me something right before she died," he said. He glanced at Kitty again. They'd decided to edit out the part about Jake walking in on his mother when he was a kid.

Dad's face crinkled into sadness. "What was it, son? Spit it out."

"She said, well, she said she'd..." He swallowed hard. "She said she'd had an affair years ago. With Summer's dad. And that..." He stopped. Cleared his throat. "And that Kitty..." He looked into his dad's eyes and couldn't say it.

"She told him I'm not your daughter, Dad, but I *am*," Kitty said. She scooted her chair closer to Dad and put her arms around him. "In every way that matters, I am."

Dad rested a weathered cheek on the top of Kitty's head. "Of course you're my girl," he said. "And you always will be."

Jake stared at his father. That wasn't the reaction he'd expected. Had Dad understood what they were saying?

But the emotion in Dad's eyes wasn't confusion. Just sadness.

"You're not surprised," Jake said.

Dad shook his head. "I always suspected, because of the timing. Your mother and I…we had our problems. Tried to keep them from you kids, but at the time Kitty was conceived, we were pretty far apart. Slept in separate bedrooms, in fact."

Jake had a sudden memory of Mom taking a room down the hall from Dad, saying he snored too much. Apparently, the problem had been resolved, because for most of his childhood and teen years, they'd slept in the same bed.

"So…you knew?"

Dad shook his head. "I didn't know, and I didn't want to. When she told me she was expecting, I asked her if she'd do some counseling and try to fix things between us. We saw Pastor Kevin once a week for several months. By the time you came along…" He patted Kitty's shoulder. "We were doing a lot better. And the moment I saw you, I knew you were my little girl. You always have been, and you always will be."

"Oh, Daddy." Kitty dissolved into tears, and Jake's own eyes burned a little. They all hugged and talked a little more. And Jake felt foolish, like he'd been carrying a burden he hadn't needed to carry at all.

Kitty washed her face and made fresh coffee, and they all settled down.

"What now?" Kitty asked, looking at him.

"What do you mean?"

"Now that you don't have to devote all that energy to taking care of everyone else, what do you want for *you*?"

He wanted to protect his dad and his sister, his family, as he hadn't protected his wife. But so far, it wasn't working out real well. Maybe it *was* time to lay down that burden and think about his own inner needs.

It wasn't something he'd allowed himself to consider much, but he knew the answer instantly. "I want Summer," he said. "I want to make a family of Summer and her kids. But I don't think she'll have me."

"Why not?" Dad whacked him lightly on the arm. "You may still live with your dad, like Walter Whittaker, but at least you went to trade school and you work for a living."

Kitty cracked up. "You're better looking, too. Maybe a few more gray hairs..." She reached out and plucked one from his sideburn, making him yelp. "But you clean up okay. There are possibilities."

"Summer's mad," Jake said. "Because I didn't tell her about, you know, her dad and Mom, as soon as I found out."

"So you're going to give up?" Kitty raised an eyebrow. "I never took you for a quitter."

"Don't give up if she's the woman you want," Dad said. "Even if there are ups and downs, marriage is a beautiful thing. I wouldn't give up my years with your mother for anything."

Even after what had just come to light, Dad still felt that way? Admiration filled him. His father seemed to glow with an inner goodness Jake could never hope to match.

"Don't give up," Kitty said, "but don't relax, either. She has trust issues. She needs to know you're not going to bail out on her like her husband."

"Or cheat like her father," Dad said. For the first time

in the whole conversation, there was a trace of bitterness in his tone.

"You need a plan, something special," Kitty said.

Dad nodded. "I know a little about women. I might be able to offer some ideas."

Jake put an arm around his father's stooped shoulders. "I can use all the help I can get," he said.

An hour later, Jake had a plan.

Whether it would work or not was anyone's guess.

On Sunday afternoon, as the first guests arrived for the Mother's Day Open House, Summer sucked in a deep breath and focused on her goal.

Today, she was going to set aside her personal worries and concentrate on creating a good Mother's Day for others, and on healing and restoring the Holiday Haven Guesthouse and the men who lived here, Jake and Mr. Wright.

Her own heart was full. The kids had brought her breakfast in bed, a pretty plate of coffee cake and scrambled eggs with a little vase of daisies beside it. It had all been so good that she wasn't shocked to hear they'd had "just a little help" from Mr. Wright.

They didn't mention Jake helping, which caused her a tiny twinge of sadness. But Jake had been awfully busy the past few days, making extra visits into town and talking on his phone while he paced around the yard. She didn't know what he was working on, and he hadn't shared it.

Which might mean he was upset with her for how quickly she'd judged him. That was fair. She wanted to find a time to apologize. Maybe today, after the guests went home.

She greeted the first arrivals, dressed casually as the invitations and flyers had suggested. She directed the men and kids to the back deck, where Jake, Wyatt, Rylee, Mason and

Mr. Wright were prepared to receive them and keep them busy and happy.

Kitty set down her plate of dainty snacks and hurried over to greet a woman who'd come alone. They spoke for a moment, and then Kitty guided her off toward the relaxation room they'd set up. Kitty was good that way. She got it. The two of them had been talking a lot in the past few days, catching up on their lives, finding their tentative way as sisters.

It was one of several reasons she didn't really want to move out of the guesthouse anymore. She loved living next door to Kitty and Mason.

Once there was a group of women talking happily in the kitchen, enjoying snacks and drinks, Summer went outside to check on the men and kids. The smell of bratwurst and burgers drifted over from the grill, manned by Mr. Wright and one of his friends. Jake and the dads were down in the yard, tossing footballs with school-aged kids. She had a moment's panic when she didn't see Rylee, but Mr. Wright caught her eye and pointed toward one of the tables, where Rylee and a couple of other preschoolers had draped tablecloths to create a playhouse.

She turned to go back inside and nearly ran into another mom, Margery, a woman she knew slightly because her son was in Wyatt's class. She and her son must have just arrived. "Hey, Wyatt," she called down into the crowd of kids playing on the lawn. "Come show Brenden what's going on."

Wyatt started to object, but a word from Jake sent him trudging up the stairs. He greeted the other boy as Summer re-introduced herself to the mom.

"Oh, I remember who you are," Margery said. "I heard the saddest thing about you, that your husband wasn't really your husband after all. Honestly, it sounded like a made-for-

TV movie. I'm sorry you and your kids had to cope with that. You must have felt awful about yourself!"

Summer tilted her head, studying the woman's face. She couldn't tell whether the comments were meant to be sympathetic or cruel. But it didn't matter, she decided. "That's about him, not about me," she said. "Thankfully, there are better, kinder people in the world, and that's who I'm focusing on."

"Oh." Margery looked disconcerted. "Well, that's smart, I guess."

Wyatt nudged her, and she realized that the two boys had heard every word Margery had said. Would it lead to Wyatt getting teased?

"Can we go play now?" he asked. He sounded totally unconcerned. Just the way Summer had felt upon hearing Margery's remarks. Clearly, Wyatt was taking his cues from her. All the more reason to be glad she was getting things straight in her head.

Wyatt had come a long way, and so had she, since arriving in River Haven.

Last Tuesday's dinner with Kitty and Gemma had pushed her away from blaming herself for Chuck's actions. Several hours of thinking and praying about the situation had lifted her out of the mire of it. When Chuck had called yesterday, asking to arrange a time to visit with the kids, she'd agreed they could do that, sometime this summer.

Hadn't told the kids yet, though. Chuck had shown himself to be unreliable, and she didn't want to set them up for disappointment.

A couple of the dads came over to her. "Nice event," one of them said.

The other pointed down to where Jake stood, coaching a couple of kids about throwing technique. "Jake Wright is a good guy," he said. "Known him forever. He's honest through and through."

"One of our small-town boys," the other man said. "Small-town values, just like we need in this country."

She smiled and thanked them for coming, then headed back inside. She steered Margery toward the kitchen and then peeked in the door of the respite room.

Two women occupied a pair of comfortable chairs, chatting in the lamplight. Soft instrumental music played. When she looked closer, she realized that each woman held a kitten in her lap. The babies Rylee had chosen had come up to live in the house just this past week.

She went back into the kitchen and made sure everyone had tea or punch or snacks. A white-haired woman came over to her. "I really like Jake Wright, who owns this place," she said. "You know, he cleaned my gutters for me without being asked. Just saw that they needed it and brought a ladder over. He and his dad are the salt of the earth."

"They're great," Summer said.

"I'd trust them with my grandkids anytime," the woman added, and then another woman came up and greeted her, and they walked off to chat.

Wyatt's teacher arrived with her husband and kids, and thanked Summer for having them. "I always loved this event," she said. "A little break from kids is just what the doctor ordered. Jake's mom knew what she was doing, and it's great that Jake is keeping up the tradition." She paused, then added, "I've known Jake for years. He's solid. A great guy."

"He is." Summer frowned as she got the woman a beverage. Was it her imagination, or were a weirdly large number of people telling her how great Jake was?

As the party wound down, two more people approached her and found ways to mention that Jake was trustworthy, that they'd known him their whole lives, that he was a great man with great character. They seemed utterly sincere, but still…

Finally, after they'd said goodbye to the last guests and started cleaning up the wreckage, Mr. Wright came over. He put an arm around her. "This has been great," he said. "Just like the old days. And Jake did a good job with the kids. He's always been responsible like that."

"Sure has," Kitty said, chiming in. "He's the perfect uncle for Mason. He'd be a great dad, too."

Summer dried her hands on a dish towel and then put them on her hips. "Will someone tell me what's going on? I know Jake's a good guy. If I didn't, though, at least ten other people have told me how trustworthy he is."

Kitty looked over her shoulder and smiled, and Summer turned to see Jake in the doorway. He'd braced his arms on either side of it, and in his short-sleeved T-shirt… Wow. Those shoulders and biceps! It was obvious that Jake worked in a physical job.

"Come take a break with me?" he asked, looking directly at Summer. "The cleanup crew just got here."

"Cleanup crew?" She looked over at Kitty, who shrugged.

"High school kids," Jake clarified. "I figured everyone would be tired after the event. Dad's got Rylee and Wyatt and Mason in the front room, watching a movie. You should join them," he added, nodding at Kitty.

This was starting to feel distinctly like a setup, but of what kind, Summer hadn't a clue. She and Jake got the teenagers started on cleanup. "If you have any questions," Jake told them, "my dad and sister will answer them. They're in there." Then he held out his arm to Summer. "Let's walk down to the river," he said. "I have something to show you."

When they got there, Summer gasped. There was a

wooden swinging bench that sat facing the river. It looked like an Amish design, simple, except for the heart carved into the middle of the seat back. "It's beautiful," she said. "It'll make the guesthouse that much more romantic."

He nodded. "Try it out. It's comfortable." He sat down on one side and nodded toward the other.

Hesitantly, Summer sat down. They weren't touching, but it was close quarters and she could feel the warmth of his arm.

Late-afternoon sunshine made the air seem almost golden. A pair of ducks flew in, quacking, and landed neatly on the river. Rich, moist air gave the scent of springtime.

Jake used his foot to swing them gently. "I can move this anywhere," he said, "although I hope to live on this river for the rest of my life."

"Okaaaay," she said slowly. "But that comment seems random. Lots of comments have seemed random today. What's going on?"

"I figured you'd notice." He shifted until his arm was along the back of the seat, and now she definitely felt the warmth of him. "Summer, you have every reason not to trust people, especially men, after what you've been through with your dad and your husband. I didn't want you to have to take my word that I wouldn't let you down, so I wanted you to hear it from a lot of other people."

"You set this up?"

He nodded.

"You called all of those people?" Given that Jake was the strong and silent type, she was amazed.

"Called, or visited," he said. "Asked them to tell you the truth about me."

She slid over so she could face him. "And you did that because..."

"Guess I got ahead of myself," he said, his eyes crinkling with a smile. "Look, let me just say it. I've fallen in love with you."

Summer stared at him, her heart beating so hard she couldn't speak.

"You're so happy all the time," he said. "Even when you have a lot of worries, you're just a happy person. Your parents named you right, calling you Summer. You're like summertime."

It was the nicest thing anyone had ever said to her.

"And you're a good, kind person. You're good to your kids, and you've been good to my dad and me. I admire how you pick yourself up and go on, but listen…you won't have to do that with me. I've got your back. I'm here for the duration if you'll have me."

Finally, she found her voice. "What are you saying, exactly?"

He reached in his pocket, and her mouth fell open. He stopped and shook his head. "It's not what you think. It's not a ring. Well, it is, but not…" He pulled out his hand, with something in it. He kept the object enclosed in his large fist.

A goldfinch landed on the top of a nearby thistle, studied them quizzically as it swayed, and then flew off.

Jake took her hand and put something in it, keeping his hand closed over hers. "It's a kind of a hippie ring," he said. "Not even a new one. It's been in the guesthouse lost and found forever."

"Okay," she said, confused.

"It seemed, well, I felt like it would be arrogant for me to pick out an engagement ring. I don't know what you'd like, and I don't know if you'll say yes."

Summer stared at him. It seemed like, in a roundabout

way, he was asking her to…what? Marry him? Get engaged to him? Have a hippie-type relationship with him?

"Look at it," he urged, and let go of her hand.

She opened hers, and her hand flew to her mouth. "It's just like the mood ring my mom wore."

"It might actually *be* hers," he said. "I thought it could be sort of a holding piece, while you decide if you'll have me. And if you do decide yes, then we can shop for whatever kind of ring you'd like."

He'd thought it all through in his quiet, methodical way. It was totally unlike her previous marriage proposal, and it was so very Jake. Her heart swelled with an emotion she couldn't name, not yet.

She slipped the ring onto her right hand and studied it. "Look, it's blue," she said.

He held her hand, gently and carefully, as if she were a treasure he wanted to keep safe. "It's blue and getting darker. Is that good or bad?"

"Good. Very good." She smiled up at him, her heart pounding in a steady rhythm. "Wow, Jake, you're kind of bowling me over here."

"You don't have to say anything. Or do anything. I just wanted you to know."

She leaned forward and kissed him on the lips, lightly, stopping his words. "I need to take my time, because of the kids. But I really appreciate all you've done for us. From giving me a job and a place to live, to teaching Wyatt to throw a baseball, to helping me find them when they were lost… and Jake, I'm sorry I judged you so harshly, before. You were only trying to do the right thing."

"I didn't go about it right. And you should know that's par for the course with me. I screw up on a regular basis."

A man who admits that he screws up? Priceless, she thought.

"I make a lot of mistakes too," she said. Peace flowed into her now, steady as the river in front of them. It was a Mother's Day she'd never, ever forget. She scooted over next to him and wrapped her arms around his neck. "I think… I'd like to give this a try."

She heard a train on the tracks across the road. Saw a pair of squirrels chasing each other up a tree.

And then it was only Jake she could see, only Jake's warmth she could feel.

As they kissed, her last rational thought was that God had surely brought all of this together. It was so beautiful and so perfect, it could only be from Him.

Epilogue

Two weeks after Mother's Day, Summer was still riding high on the joy of being with Jake. An official couple. Engaged, even.

It was Memorial Day, and she was getting set up for a family picnic. They'd all agreed to forget about the fact that the guesthouse was opening next weekend. For this one day, they'd set aside work and celebrate their togetherness. Kitty and Mason would be over soon with desserts. Gemma, who had no family, was joining them with her daughter, and had promised to bring kid-friendly pasta. And of course, there would be Mr. Wright, and Rylee, and Wyatt.

And Jake. Wonderful Jake.

He was a quiet man, down to earth. But she was learning that he was also deeply romantic. Most days, he brought her flowers, sometimes a big bouquet, and sometimes a single rosebud. When she protested that she was running out of vases, he'd obligingly switched to chocolate. He was affectionate, and he didn't mind if people saw it or even teased him about it. "You're my woman, and I'm proud of you," he said simply.

As she spread a red-and-white checkered tablecloth over the long picnic table, she couldn't keep the smile off her face. It was going to be a big group, the kind of family she'd always wanted. She couldn't fault her parents for the exciting childhood they'd given her, but holidays had been lonely with just the three of them. That was why they'd loved coming to the Holiday Haven Guesthouse, and that was what she and Jake and Mr. Wright wanted to re-create: a place where lonely people could come to spend holidays with a sense of family and community.

The guesthouse was all painted and cleaned. They'd gotten new furniture as needed, but they'd kept the same whimsical, creative touches Jake's mother had put onto the place.

She and Jake had spent time talking about their parents, and she suspected they'd spend a good deal more. It was strange having to think about your parents as sinners, but like the pastor always emphasized, everyone was a sinner. You had only to read the Bible to know that history was full of flawed characters who constantly made mistakes.

God still used them. And God had worked their parents' affair for good, as evidenced by Kitty, who now ran up the stairs of the deck. Mr. Wright came out of the guesthouse at the same moment, and they hugged each other. It seemed to Summer that the revelation that they weren't blood relatives had actually strengthened their bond.

Summer went inside and was putting the finishing touches on a platter of deviled eggs when there was a knock on the guesthouse's front door. She wiped her hands and went to answer it.

Her heart almost dropped to the floor. "Chuck? What are you doing here?"

"I should have given warning, I know," he said. "But we were passing through, and I thought I'd take the chance to say a quick hello."

"We?" She looked past him toward the SUV he'd apparently arrived in. Had he truly had the gall to bring his other family to see Summer and the kids?

"They're not here," he said quickly. "They're back at the hotel."

She looked at the man she'd once loved and felt nothing. Nothing except irritation that he'd come to rain on their party.

"Daddy!" Rylee came running out and grabbed onto Chuck's leg.

He knelt down and hugged her, burying his face in her hair. "I've missed you, sweetie."

Wyatt came down the stairs. When he saw his father, he froze.

Automatically, Summer walked over and put a hand on his shoulder. "Your dad surprised us with a visit," she said, keeping her voice neutral. "Do you want to say hi? It's up to you." She planned to facilitate the kids' relationship with their father as best she could, but she wasn't going to force a display of affection that would surely be false.

Wyatt's forehead wrinkled. It had been several months since he'd seen his father, and he was old enough to understand the nuances in a way Rylee couldn't.

Chuck stood, and looked straight at Wyatt. "Hello, son," he said. "How's it going?"

Summer kept her hand on Wyatt's shoulder, her stomach churning. This was a situation she had no precedent for.

Rylee let go of her father's hand and ran into the front room. "Mr. Grandpa! Mr. Grandpa! Come meet my daddy!"

Mr. Wright did come in, but he didn't shake the hand Chuck offered. "You have a couple of great kids here," he said, his voice flat. The unspoken rest of the sentence was loud and clear: *and you don't deserve them.*

Rylee ran back and forth between the two men, talking enough to fill the silence between them. Wyatt ran back up the stairs, and Summer winced. She wasn't going to make him hang out with his father when the visit was so unexpected, but for him to just leave without saying a word had to be painful for Chuck. And pretty awkward for the rest of them.

A moment later, though, Wyatt returned with Jake. "Um, that's my dad," he said to Jake, pointing.

Jake squeezed Wyatt's shoulder and then came down the steps to stand by Summer. "Were you invited?" he asked Chuck.

"Me and Summer talked about it," Chuck said, sounding defensive.

Summer finally found her voice. "We discussed your visiting the kids, but we didn't make a specific plan. In the future, you'll need to prearrange it with me." Thanks to the example of Jake and Mr. Wright, she managed to keep her tone even.

"Yeah, sure, of course." Chuck rubbed the back of his neck, his face red. Clearly, this visit wasn't going as he'd hoped or expected.

"If you'd like to, you may show your dad around the lawn and deck," Summer said to the kids. She didn't want him inside. But she'd been reading up on how to handle co-parenting with someone you didn't much like, and the consensus was: try to show as much respect as if you were still married to them.

"Come on!" Rylee started out the door. Wyatt followed his sister, slowly, sidling past Chuck without touching him.

It was a little heartbreaking, considering how Wyatt had tried to please his father as a younger kid. Tried to get the attention that hadn't been forthcoming.

Chuck started to follow Rylee, but Jake caught up in two long strides and stepped in front of him, blocking his path. "You can see your kids if Summer says so. But I'm looking out for them now, and for Summer, too. If you get out of line, you'll have me to deal with."

"And me." Mr. Wright walked forward to stand beside Jake.

Limp with all the emotions, Summer let herself sink down onto the steps. She could take care of herself and manage Chuck, of course. But that wall of strong, protective manhood between her and the man who'd betrayed her definitely felt welcome.

She closed her eyes. *Thank You, Father.* She'd found a family for her kids, so much better than what she'd had with Chuck. Everywhere she looked, she saw God's hand on their lives.

Jake planned to be a father to Summer's kids. Mr. Wright was already a surrogate grandfather. They'd shown their love and caring almost since the day Summer and the kids had arrived, when Mr. Wright had taken Wyatt fishing and Jake had let them stay.

It wasn't blood that made a family, it was love. Love in action.

Summer looked down at her hands. She wore the mood ring Jake had given her on her right hand and her new, gorgeous engagement ring on her left. She wondered if Chuck had noticed it.

Didn't matter.

She and Jake had decided to stay in the guesthouse while it got up and running, meanwhile building their own house in a lot on the other side of the auto shop. They'd be right down the street from Mr. Wright, Kitty, Gemma and the kids.

They hadn't set a wedding date yet, but Jake was pushing for sooner rather than later.

Jake walked over, sat on the steps, and put his arm around

her. Mr. Wright stood sentinel in the doorway, watching Chuck and the kids.

Summer leaned against her fiancé and felt him kiss the top of her head. Contentment filled her.

Her parents had shown her the world, or at least the country, but it turned out that happiness was right here, in River Haven.

She stood and held out a hand to Jake. "Come on, let's finish getting dinner together."

Jake followed her into the kitchen and kissed her thoroughly. Soon enough Chuck was gone, and the kids were welcoming their friends. Mr. Wright and Jake got the grill going, and Kitty, Gemma, and Summer worked and laughed around the kitchen.

Life would go on in this comfortable way. Now, Summer felt confident in it. Picking up a tray of shucked corn on the cob, she headed outside to the man she loved.

* * * * *

Dear Reader,

Thank you for visiting River Haven! I'm so excited about this new series, set in a guesthouse in a small, Western Pennsylvania river town. It's actually modeled on a real guesthouse I visited in Confluence, Pennsylvania, close to where I live. As soon as I saw the haphazard structure, the big deck and the beautiful river, I knew I'd found a home for my next set of Love Inspired books.

The "holiday" part of the Holiday Haven Guesthouse is wishful thinking on my part. My family is small, and sometimes when we can't get together with out-of-state relatives, it's just me and my daughter on holidays. Well, and our goofy pets. We have fun, but I sometimes think it would be nice to spend the holidays surrounded by a crowd of friendly people. That's what the Holiday Haven Guesthouse is all about.

Jake and Summer are good, hardworking people. They're perfect together…but their troubled pasts make it hard for them to make a commitment and connect. After I figured out their backstories, I had to find a way for them to get past their issues and fall in love. And there were Mr. Wright, Wyatt and Rylee, fun and lively and eager to help Jake and Summer make a family together.

You can expect to see all the characters from this book when the guesthouse gears up for a big Fourth of July celebration. That book comes out in June 2026. I sure am hoping that either Kitty or Gemma finds love! Which one do you think should be first?

Check out my website and send me a note letting me know. While you're there, join my newsletter to stay up-to-date on all my books. I do fun giveaways in the newsletter every month, too! Find me at *www.leetobinmcclain.com.*

Happy Mother's Day!
Lee